Shared by Her Bodyguards

By Cassie Cole

Copyright © 2019 Juicy Gems Publishing

All rights reserved. No part of this publication may be reproduced, distributed, or transmitted in any form without prior consent of the author.

Edited by Dorothy Eller

Interested in joining Cassie's exclusive mailing list to receive deals on Reverse Harem Romance? Sign up here: http://eepurl.com/dFpnSz

Books by Cassie Cole

Broken In
Drilled
Five Alarm Christmas
All In
Triple Team
Shared by her Bodyguards

1

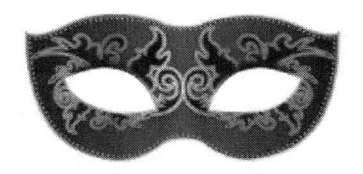

Ethan

I unlocked the door to the hotel room. A *stranger's* hotel room.

Because as one of Washington D.C.'s most expensive male escorts, I was hired to be here.

The door creaked as it opened slowly. I took my time walking inside and allowing it to swing closed behind me, then made sure to turn the deadbolt loud enough that whichever client was inside would hear the click, then did the same with the chain lock. It would make them feel like there was no going back. It was part of the anticipation.

Part of my job.

My footsteps echoed heavily on the floor as I walked down the hall of the suite. Slowly, building up the suspense. I could smell perfume in the air, flowery and sweet, bringing with it memories of past encounters in hotels like this. A *nice* hotel, with expensive-looking paintings on the wall and dark, floral-print wallpaper underneath. That narrowed it down to only a couple of my clients.

I rounded the corner to see who had paid for my company tonight.

She was seated on the edge of the bed, one long leg crossed over the other. She wore black lingerie, stockings that went halfway up her thighs before clipping into garters, and a matching push-up bra that made her already full breasts stand up wonderfully. Tattoos ran down her right arm; a flock of tiny black birds taking flight toward her fingers.

Yet a mask covered her face from eyes to mouth.

It was an expensive venetian mask, charcoal-colored with gold embroidery around the outside. The eye holes were wide and cat-like, but fabric was sewn behind them so I couldn't see her eyes.

Some of the people in this town had strange fetishes. As a male escort, it was my job to fulfill them.

My heart did a backflip when I recognized the mask. It was *her*. I still didn't know what her face looked like, but this would be our fourth time together. My cock rose at the sight of her. In the warm light of the hotel lamps she was stunning in a way that stirred something primal within me.

With a wolfish smile I walked slowly toward the bed, landing on my heels so she could feel my approach. Her chest heaved with anticipation as I stopped directly in front of her. The woman's perfect porcelain skin practically trembled as she waited for our evening to begin. Waiting for what I would do next.

I paused to admire her, and to draw out the anticipation. I was going to enjoy every bit of this as much as she was.

I pawed her legs apart, which drew a soft gasp. Then I grabbed the fabric of her panties with both hands and ripped a hole in the middle. Her file told me she liked that. The soft moans escaping from her lips told me, too.

Standing back up, I took my time undressing in front of her while her legs were spread on the edge of the bed. Like I had all the time in the world. I made her listen to the swishing sound of my tie being pulled slowly through my shirt collar, and the sound of buttons rubbing against cloth as I unbuttoned my shirt. Every tooth of my zipper clicking open, and the rasp of my belt being removed with a flourish. By the time I was nude I could see she was as wet as could be.

I wished she could see me too. I maintained a chiseled body for my clients, and her mask ruined all my hard work. Since she was effectively blind, I took her hand and placed it on my chest, then guided it over my body. Letting her feel the mounds of my pecs, the swollen muscles in my arm, the lines of my chiseled abs. I wanted her to picture the powerful man who was about to ravage her.

The last thing I did was pull her hand down toward my raging hard cock. But I only brushed her hand against it rather than let her grab hold, then I tossed her hand aside. She leaned back on her hands on the bed. Waiting.

How was I going to take her tonight? She liked it a little rough. So did I. If not for the mask obscuring her mouth I might have straddled her face and fucked her throat, holding her down on my thick manhood until she gagged. I didn't need her file to tell me she was the kind of woman who would get off on that. I tried imagining what her lips looked like underneath the fabric...

"You know what I'm going to do to you tonight?" I asked in a deep, authoritarian voice.

She shook her head. In our handful of times together, she'd never spoken.

"What I'm going to do to you," I said slowly, "is whatever the fuck I want."

She sucked in her breath.

I pushed her down onto the bed, *hard*. Then I flipped her over so that her plump ass was up in the air, the thong hidden within those delicious round cheeks. She tried to spread her legs but I pressed them together like unbroken chopsticks, then climbed on top of her, planting my knees on either side of her thighs to lock her in place. I took hold of my cock and wedged it down between her thighs, guiding it up toward her wet slit, but stopping just before giving it to her. She tried to spread her legs again but I kept my knees firmly in place to stop her. The feel of her skin against mine stirred an animal-like desire in my chest.

She trembled with anticipation.

I paused here, drawing it out even though I desperately wanted her as much as she wanted me. I was going to fuck her to the edge of what she could handle.

When her excitement reached its peak, I forced my cock inside. That's how she liked it: hard and rough, no wasted time getting acclimated. She moaned loudly through her mask as my cock disappeared inside her pussy in a quick, forceful thrust.

She tried to push up onto her knees into the doggy style position, but I planted my strong hands on her back and shoved her down onto her belly. Practically *throwing* her down, much harder than I needed to. That made her moan even louder, and I put a hand on the back of her head to push it deeper into the flawless hotel pillow.

I held her flat on the bed while I remained on my knees, then grabbed her waist for leverage and began fucking her hard from behind. Her pussy gripped my cock so tight I had to take a deep breath and remind myself *she* was the client. Even muffled by the mask, her cries of pleasure were delicious and deep. She reached a hand back to touch my chest but I snatched it out of the air and pressed it down on the bed. The force of that sent a tremble of pleasure through her body, with moans that undulated like music.

I crashed my cock into her again and again, bouncing my little sex kitten on the bed with each thrust as I had my way with her.

I admired how she looked underneath me, accepting my raging cock like a good girl. The muscles in her back flexed as she squirmed, until I planted my palm in between her shoulder blades and held her down. Her hair was tied up underneath the mask but a stray lock fell out onto the back of her long neck. Dark blonde, the color of honey. Goddamn, I wished I could rip the mask off and get a look at the face of the woman I was ravaging, to grab a fistful of her hair and yank her head back while I fucked her for all I was worth.

She was squirming more and more now, her moans of ecstasy quickening in that wonderful way that told me how close she was. I fell forward on her, flattening her entire body underneath mine, giving her shoulder a gentle nibble, running my teeth up toward her neck. Only now did I move my legs, sliding them in between her thighs and allowing her to spread her legs wide for me. She was so wet I could feel her juices collecting in my pubic hair, evidence that I was doing a great job.

But now it was time to *really* earn my paycheck.

"You like being fucked by a stranger?" I growled

into her ear.

She bobbed her masked head up and down.

"You take my cock well, you dirty little whore."

The moans of pleasure intensified.

I wrapped my left arm underneath her belly, and my right arm around her neck. Taking a stranglehold on her beautiful body with my muscle, like a python constricting its prey. I pumped up and down on her firm ass, burying my throbbing cock deeper inside of her from this new angle. Hitting her most sensitive places. She moaned louder and squirmed but I tightened my arms around her, allowing my bicep to squeeze up against her throat. Only a little pressure for now—testing to see if she liked this.

From the way she reacted, she definitely did.

"Your juicy little cunt is mine," I rasped as I picked up speed. I almost had her. "Is your cunt mine?"

She nodded as vigorously as she could with my arm around her neck. What might have been a muffled, "yes," turned into a cry of ecstasy. I could feel her climax nearing, like the rumble of a motorcycle you could sense but not yet see.

I went in for the kill.

I moved forward a small amount, which changed the angle ever so slightly. Now each thrust rubbed the head of my cock against her forward wall, that perfect friction against her most sensitive place. The scream of pleasure she let out was like pure heaven to my ears.

I moved my left hand up around one of her breasts, and loosened my right arm around her neck—but only so I could take hold of it with my fingers. I gripped her neck tightly, squeezing my fingers into her perfect porcelain flesh.

She came with her whole body; she screamed from behind her mask and her entire back shuddered underneath me like an earthquake. Her pussy lips clenched so tight around my cock that it dragged me into my own ragged orgasm. My moans joined hers, a rumbling deep within my chest. Her pussy gripped me as tightly as my fingers gripped her neck. We howled together in a duet of passion as I filled her to the brim with my hot seed.

We lay there for a long moment, the silence in the aftermath deafening compared to the delirious noises we'd been making moments before. Two bodies pressed tightly together, our rapid breaths in perfect synchronicity.

I let go of her neck, leaving red marks where my fingers had been. Her body heaved with deep breaths as I pushed up onto my knees, then allowed my cock to slide out of her. It rested against her perfect ass, glistening from our combined juices.

Fuck, I thought.

I wished I could stay there forever. To remove the mask and taste her lips as we cuddled and kissed on the sheets, exploring our bodies for the rest of the night. I wanted to look deep into her eyes when she came, to see the fire within caused by my love.

But that's not what her client file required. I had very specific instructions. Before, during, *and* after.

I gave one cheek a hard smack. It made a satisfying sound, punctuated by the soft squeak from her mouth. "You have a good, tight pussy," I growled as I climbed off the bed, fingers raking along her leg. "Next time maybe I'll take you in the ass. See how tight *that* is."

"Mmm," she grunted, turning over and reclining on the bed, arms extended over her head as she stretched.

I was tempted to push the limits of our arrangement. To offer her another go, on the house. I didn't want to leave just yet. I wanted to do so many more things to this woman whose face I'd never seen. I was one of Washington D.C.'s most expensive male escorts, but all I wanted was *her*.

It took all of my willpower to get dressed and leave without another word.

2

Elizabeth

I lay on the bed, too satisfied to move until long after he was gone.

That was what I'd been looking forward to all week. Just the thing an overworked, stressed senator from Ohio needed to help release a little bit of tension from the job.

Being a public figure had its drawbacks. I couldn't scratch my sexual itch on normal dates, or on a random Tinder hookup. Photos would be taken. Op-eds would be written. Paparazzi would begin hounding me at all hours of the day. It would be the end of my career.

So I paid handsome men to satisfy my insatiable sexual desire in hotel rooms while I wore a mask.

I knew what Ethan looked like, even if I couldn't see him during the act itself. I'd picked him out of a digital catalog, after all. All the male escorts in this town were solid 10s, bodybuilders and former athletes chiseled with hard muscle looking to earn an extra buck. Ethan was as sexy as they came. He had an Owen Wilson thing going on, with blond hair and a nose that might have been broken once or twice. A muscle-riddled surfer dude with a knack for taking hold of his clients and fucking them to within an inch of their lives.

I'd been doing this every couple of weeks for about a year, and usually I picked a different escort every week. But this was... how many times with Ethan? Four, or five? It wouldn't be the last time, either. I knew that with as much certainty as I knew anything in my life. Within a few days that itch would need to be scratched again, and then it would be a sixth time, and maybe a seventh if he kept spicing things up...

"Lord have mercy," I whispered to myself on the bed. The way he'd squeezed his arm around my neck, with just the right amount of force, had struck every erogenous nerve in my body. Ethan was definitely worth every penny. If Ethan was even his real name.

I tore off the mask and tossed it on the bed. I wished it wasn't necessary. I wished I could stare up into my lover's eyes while he fucked me every which way, on the bed and bent over the chair and up against the wall...

I wished things didn't have to be so secretive.

I locked the door from the inside, took my time showering, and then left the hotel. I used the stairs and went out the back door, just in case Ethan decided to get a drink in the hotel bar or was waiting somewhere for me to leave. I didn't *think* he would try to learn my identity to blackmail me, but you could never be too careful in this town. Everyone was looking for leverage.

The back alley was dark and slushy with half-melted snow, but it was the only way to avoid potential photographers. Although Ethan might not try anything, the paparazzi were another story. They'd shown up unexpectedly outside restaurants after key senate bills before. Fortunately, no cameras flashed as I exited the alley, walked two blocks to the parking garage where my car waited, and drove home in peace.

My apartment was on the upper side of D.C., close to Silver Springs, Maryland. One of six three-story condos crammed together on a block. I rarely went back to Ohio these days, so this was my home for 90% of the year.

It felt cold and lonely, even with the heat cranked up to keep the winter chill at bay.

I placed my venetian mask on the mantle above the fireplace. "Until next time."

I glanced at my watch. I wished I could stay up

and relax a little. Watch some TV or read a book, something to unwind after the long day—and exciting night—I'd had. But tomorrow was going to be just as long, as was the day after that. There were no short days for a United States senator.

"Thanks for the good time, Ethan," I said as I crawled into my big, empty bed.

3

Elizabeth

My body woke itself up at 3:25, five minutes before my alarm. I pulled on tight running leggings and my light windbreaker and ignored the burst of frigid air that smacked me in the face when I opened the front door.

A morning jog helped me wake up more than any cup of coffee. Working up a sweat, getting my blood flowing. With all the craziness waiting for me on the Hill, this was the only time I had to myself. Everything in the world was calm and peaceful, even if only for 30 minutes.

Plus, appearances mattered for a politician.

Especially for a female politician. Keeping myself in reasonably good health was as important as fundraising.

My morning on Capitol Hill was busy and overcrowded with work. I was on the Senate Finance Committee, which met promptly at 8:00, but I liked to get into my senate office early to get a head start on the small stuff, like responding to constituents who had called or emailed my office. I had a team of interns who answered most of my emails, but I still liked to respond to a handful every day. To keep my pulse on my constituents back in Ohio. To remember that *I* worked for *them*, and not the other way around.

The Finance Committee dealt with the various revenue generating matters of the federal government: taxes, tariffs, and other matters relating to customs or ports of entry. Most people would find it boring, tedious work, but not me. Numbers were my *jam*. I was the kind of woman who liked to audit accounting books for fun, spending an entire day trying to make the numbers properly add up. Not only did I enjoy it, but I was good at it, too. It wasn't often a young senator found herself on a committee so early in her career.

Like all days on the Hill, this one flew by. Our committee was interrupted several times when votes on the senate floor were announced, requiring us to rush inside, verbally cast our vote, and then return. I ate my lunch while listening to the testimony from a port of entry manager who said entrants weren't properly declaring all items upon entering the United States, and who insisted our customs forms be modified. Then the afternoon was spent back on the senate floor listening to deliberations on half a dozen bills. The bills all had near unanimous support from both parties, but certain senators still wanted to get up and say their peace. Getting as much time in front of the CSPAN cameras as possible. Footage that could later be used in campaign ads.

I glanced at my watch. I was counting down the minutes until we adjourned for the day because I had a meeting with my campaign manager this afternoon. One I'd been looking forward to for weeks. The opposition research we had ordered had finally come back.

Eventually a wooden gavel banged against the table, calling an end to today's senate session. I gathered my laptop and papers and quickly shuffled out of the chamber.

I chit-chatted with two other senators while walking down the hall. Everyone was friendly when we were out of session, even members of opposing parties. Most senators had families. I was one of the few bachelorettes on the Hill, but I still enjoyed asking others how their kids were. If little Johnny had made the debate team, or if Suzy was still swimming.

I almost didn't notice the Capitol Policeman standing at attention in the hallway. They were everywhere, silently keeping us safe, but there was something different about this cop. Most stared straight ahead, or gave a respectful nod or greeting. But this guy? He *leered*. His eyes followed me as I approached, and he grinned like he knew me. And then, as I passed him, he made a grunting noise. The kind a guy makes when his juicy steak arrives at the table.

"Excuse me?" I said, stopping. The other senators with me, two women and one man, stopped too. "Is there something I can help you with?"

The cop's smile reached his eyes. "There's *plenty* you could help me with," he said in a deep, suggestive voice.

One of the other senators almost choked on her coffee. Another snickered with incredulity.

I took a good look at him. He had a thin black beard and messy dark hair underneath his hat. He'd broken uniform protocol by rolling up his sleeves, revealing colorful tattoos on his muscular forearms. I could tell by the way his uniform fit that the rest of his body was also covered with muscle. His eyes held a sexy promise as he stared back coolly.

He was gorgeous in every way. Like a delicious stripper version of a policeman. But he was also young. 25 at most, a decade my junior.

I might have laughed the whole thing off and given him a flirty comment of my own, but the other senators were watching. Waiting to see what I would do. I fixed the officer with a cool stare.

"What's your badge number?" I asked. I didn't

intend to report him, but I wanted to make him sweat.

But this guy? He only grinned back at me. "Take a closer look for yourself."

Now that he'd called my bluff, I had to follow through. I pulled out my phone, leaned in, and snapped a photo of the badge on his chest. Up close his cologne smelled peppery and sweet.

"Enjoy unemployment," I said, turning away.

"You got it, sugar."

I paused. "The proper way to address me is *Senator O'Hare*."

"You got it, Senator O'Hare," he said with that same smile. I felt it on my backside all the way down the hall.

"There aren't many Capitol Policeman leering at me!" said Senator Hitchens with a laugh. She was 62 and had been serving the people of Rhode Island for almost 30 years. "Enjoy it while it lasts."

"I'll try," I muttered. I felt annoyed by the interaction... But only a little bit. The flirting was almost a welcome change from the men who looked at female politicians like we were vipers, unsure whether they should point and laugh at us or run away screaming. It was nice to be appreciated as a physical person sometimes. Even if my position meant I could never *really* enjoy the attention.

Megan, my bubbly campaign manager, was waiting in my office. "About time!" she said.

I closed the door and rounded my desk. "Carlson was droning on and on about the security bill. You know how it is."

She grimaced, then waved it all away. "First of all, happy birthday." She tossed a card onto the desk. "You need to come to Frankie's Pub tonight at 7:00."

I groaned. "Not a surprise party."

"The staff insisted," Megan said. "I promised them I would find a way to lure you out. All you have to do is make an appearance."

"I hate surprise parties!"

"They're easy. Show up, act surprised, have a drink, then go home knowing there are people in your life who care about you."

Those people didn't care about me. Not *really*. They were coworkers and staff who really just wanted to get on my good side by sucking up. Everyone was always angling for favors in this town.

"Fine," I said. "But only because 35 is the most important birthday of my life."

We grinned at each other.

"Speaking of that, people are starting to talk," Megan said. "Our secret isn't going to be a secret much longer."

"Let them talk. Light rumors never hurt anyone. If anything, it helps build up the suspense for when we finally *do* announce." I paused and waited. "Well? Did we get it?"

She pulled out a thick folder from her bag. Although she'd tossed my card on the desk, this item she placed as carefully as a newborn child.

"The third party oppo research is here."

I grabbed it, feeling its weight. It was *thick,* like a college textbook. Did they really have this much to say about the entirety of my background?

"Did I pass?" I asked. I thought about what I'd done last night in the hotel. Those kinds of dates would need to end, soon. There would be too much scrutiny on me and my campaign. It was risky. And if the researcher had discovered evidence of those late-night meetings...

Megan smiled and opened her mouth, but then an ear-piercing siren split the air.

Both of us winced and covered our ears. "Building threat," I said.

"Bomb, or active shooter?"

"How am I supposed to know?"

As if on cue, my phone buzzed on the table. An emergency alert from the internal congressional app. I read it and said, "We're supposed to shelter in-place. A capitol policeman will let us know when it's safe."

Megan ran to the door and locked it, then came around the other side of the desk. Then we huddled together underneath its huge wooden mass.

Even though this sort of thing happened several times a month, and was always a false alarm, it was tough not to feel afraid. The political landscape was toxic these days. All it took was one nutjob with a gun and a vendetta...

Someone knocked heavily on the door. "Capitol Police. Senator O'Hare?"

I went to the door and wondered if it was the same officer who had leered at me. The voice was similar but tough to tell through the thick wood.

"Code?" I asked.

"Eisenhower."

I verified the code word on my app and opened the door. This Capitol Policeman had grey in his hair and wrinkles around his eyes, but his face was hard as stone. Surprisingly, I felt disappointed it was not the tattooed officer with the suggestive smile.

"Ma'am, please come with me to the safe room. Your staff will remain here." His hand was on his sidearm as if he might need to use it at any moment.

"Of course *I'm* expendable," Megan muttered.

"What's the problem?" I asked, although I doubted he would tell me. They never did.

He surprised me by saying, "We received a credible threat against an unspecified female senator. Please follow me."

I gave Megan one last look as I was led away.

4

Elizabeth

It was a false alarm. They always were, which I guess was the best case scenario. But I still felt frustrated when they finally let us leave since I'd missed the meeting with Megan, the one I'd been looking forward to all day. We had so much to do, so much to plan.

At least the security threat gave me an excuse to skip the surprise party at Frankie's Pub.

I opened up a bottle of wine when I got home and poured a large glass. "Happy birthday to me," I said, toasting the empty room. The silence was perfect. Senators didn't get much time to themselves.

Across the room, the venetian mask sparkled in

the light.

I tore open Megan's card. A picture of a golden retriever puppy pointed its paw up at me, with a caption that said, "Who's awesome? *You're* awesome!" I opened it and read the simple inscription on the inside:

Keep being awesome. We've got a lot of work ahead of us.
-M

The card was the kind of cheesy thing I hated. Megan knew that, which was why she'd gotten it for me. But it made me laugh, and the inscription was sweet. Short and focused, just like my campaign manager.

I pulled out my phone and texted her.

Me: Thanks for the card. It's stupid and I hate it.

Megan: Cheer up. You could be turning 75 this week, like Senator Kirono

Me: Ha ha.

Megan: Get some sleep tonight. And don't skip your morning jog tomorrow. You're always sharpest on the Hill when your endolphins are flowing.

Me: En-dolphins?

Me: I didn't realize sea mammals were part of my campaign platform!

Megan: OMG, shut up. You know I meant endorphins! Go for your jog tomorrow.

I changed into comfortable clothes, topped off my wine, and got started giving myself a birthday present.

I loved to cook. Chopping garlic, grating cheese, browning ground meat in a pan. To me it was like foreplay for dinner; the smells and tastes of all the ingredients teasing and tantalizing you before the real action. Tonight I was making my special lasagna. I rarely had time to make it for myself these days, but for my birthday I was going to make the time, even if it meant being up so late that my morning jog was a struggle.

One itch scratched last night. Another one scratched tonight. Just enough indulgence to keep me motivated and focused.

I was finishing the tomato sauce when my doorbell rang.

I froze with the wooden spatula in my hand. It wasn't Megan—I'd told her I wanted the rest of the night to myself, and she would respect that boundary. The next thing I thought of was the false alarm at the Capitol building. Maybe it wasn't a false alarm after all.

I grabbed two things from the counter: my taser,

and my congressional alarm button. I didn't want to trigger the alarm that would bring every police officer in a two mile radius down on my apartment, but I wanted the option just in case. With that in my left hand and my taser in the right, I stalked to the front door on quiet feet.

The doorbell rang again and a third time in rapid succession. Someone impatient. As I rounded the corner into my entrance hall I saw the outline of a figure through the fogged glass. It looked like a police officer holding something under one arm.

With my taser still at the ready, I threw open the door. A rush of cold air blew inside.

The Capitol Policeman looked the same as he had this afternoon, except now he held a motorcycle helmet under one arm. The cold winter air added a touch of red to his face, which somehow made him even *more* sexy than before. Now that he wasn't wearing a hat I could see that the sides of his head were shaved short, with a thicker tangle of black on top, which was currently messy because of the helmet. His motorcycle jacket covered most of his skin, but I could still see the tattoos running up the left side of his neck.

He leered at me with that same smile. Like he knew a joke the rest of the world didn't get.

"What are *you* doing here?" I demanded. "If you're here to apologize, don't bother. I'm not going to file a complaint for your behavior today."

He snorted. "I'm not here to apologize, sugar."

There was that tone again. Too familiar. I fought down the urge to appreciate it and crossed my arms. "Then why are you ringing my doorbell this late at night?"

His leather jacket creaked as he leaned back and looked up at the house with his dark eyes. "They sent me here to watch your apartment tonight. I just wanted to let you know, in case you saw my face sitting across the street and wondered how you got so lucky."

I fought down the urge to laugh in his face. He sure had a high opinion of himself. Typical from a young, cocky officer. Especially a motorcycle cop.

"My apartment doesn't need watching," I said. "Maybe try the condo four units down? Esther is 92 and could use some company."

I closed the door in his face.

I turned into the side room and watched through the slit in the curtains. He walked down my porch, then across the street to where his motorcycle was parked. He threw a leg over the bike, straddling it while looking up at my apartment. I could see his leer from here.

I closed the blinds and returned to my lasagna.

As I finished cooking the meat and sauce, and then placed the dish into the oven to bake, I could feel his presence outside. Maybe it was the wine, but it gave me a tingling sensation of being protected. I wasn't alone tonight. There was a young Capitol Policeman outside my house.

He was as cocky as could be, but that wasn't necessarily a bad thing. Much as I hated to admit it, that attitude probably would have worked on me if I was 10 years younger. Even at my current age it was working a little bit. I was a sucker for a guy with tattoos.

After a few more sips of wine, I went back to the front window. He was still straddling his bike, standing out there in the cold. How long would he watch my house? All night? He probably hadn't eaten, and I doubted he'd packed anything. Guys like him never thought ahead.

He looks like he thinks with only one thing.

Watching him stand out there, I started feeling sorry for him. Inappropriate comments aside, he was just a kid doing his job. Keeping me safe while I sat in a warm condo, treating myself to a bottle of wine and my favorite meal. It was a shitty job for him on a night like tonight, with snow threatening in those dark clouds.

I sipped my wine and wondered what other tattoos he had underneath that uniform.

5

Anthony

Fucking hell.

Out of all the politicians in Washington, I got sent to guard the ridiculously hot one.

The one I'd made a pass at today.

She was young for a senator. I'd assumed she was a campaign aide or an intern. Big fucking mistake on my part, I'll admit. But using that as an excuse would have made me look like *more* of an asshole, not less. Better to steer into the skid.

She'd answered the door wearing silk pajamas. Pants that were baggy and loose, but a top that hugged her curves more tightly. Breasts that were perky and full. She still had on the lipstick from the day which accentuated her full lips. Lips begging to be kissed. I was a sucker for a puckered red pair like that.

Fucking hell. No politician had a right to look like *that*. How was I supposed to concentrate during the day with someone like her walking around in a pencil skirt and heels? Now that I knew who she was, Senator Elizabeth O'Hare from Ohio, I wasn't even intimidated. If anything, the power she wielded made her seem even sexier. A woman with power.

I fucking *ached* for her. Literal pain deep within the sexual part of my soul. If she were someone I'd met in a bar I would have spent the entire night trying to take her home. I would've brought my A-game.

She thought she was being discrete, but I could see her peeking out the curtains at me every few minutes. Like I was a neighborhood bum who wouldn't go away. Totally unappreciative that I was out here in the dick-numbing cold. Keeping her safe.

Typical politician.

But you know what? I didn't really care. I *wanted* to keep her safe. It was my job, and I'd much rather be protecting someone like her than a wrinkled old fart who *really* took me for granted. Keeping people safe was in my blood.

The fact that it was one of the most beautiful women I'd ever seen on the Hill...

I rubbed my hands together. I had this post until I was relieved at 5:00am. I should have grabbed a sandwich from the QuikMart. Or a thermos of something hot. Yeah, soup. That's what I should have brought. I'd kill for something like that if only to keep my hands warm.

I glanced up at the apartment. She hadn't peeked out at me in a while. She'd probably already gone to bed, my frozen ass already forgotten.

"Fucking politicians," I grumbled.

"I already told you: the proper way to address me is *Senator O'Hare*."

I twisted on my bike. She stood behind me, a coat wrapped tight around her body. Even then she looked incredible, porcelain skin touched with just enough color from the cold. Rosy cheeks matching her lips.

"You look pleased with yourself," I said.

"For someone watching my apartment, you're not very observant."

"I've been watching the front door."

"But not the back, where I came around." She smiled smugly, like she'd gotten the best of me. Which, if I was being totally honest, she had.

"You came out here in the cold just to tell me I'm doing a shitty job. A valuable use of taxpayer dollars."

"I came out here to offer you some food," she leaned forward, squinting at my badge and revealing a bit of cleavage. "Officer duBois."

"I'm not hungry," I lied.

She arched an eyebrow at me. "Then I'm offering you some warmth. Come inside, have some food to be polite. Then you can go back to sulking out here like the kid who got put in timeout."

I set my jaw. "I'm not sulking."

She barked a laugh. "Okay."

She had a wonderful sparkle in her eyes. Her silky hair cascaded down her neck like a waterfall of smooth honey.

Fucking hell. I wanted to do a lot more than just watch her apartment tonight.

"Alright," I finally said. "If it'll make you feel safer, I'll keep you company inside for a little while."

She rolled her eyes and strode toward the apartment without another word. I followed close behind, tugged along by the smell of her flowery perfume.

What trouble was I going to get myself into tonight?

Fucking hell.

6

Elizabeth

I could feel him following behind me as we went into my apartment. He had a presence about him that was impossible to ignore. Boots that clomped heavily on my hardwood floor. It reminded me of Ethan walking into the hotel room last night, feet heavy with purpose.

"Take those boots off before you track dirt everywhere," I said as I went into the kitchen.

"Whatever you want, sugar."

I grabbed my wine glass off the counter and gestured. "That's the kind of thing that got you in trouble today, dude."

He grinned that knowing grin. "But it *didn't* get me in trouble."

"It's not too late for me to file a complaint," I said. "Seriously though. Is this your first day on the job, or do you really think you can get away with addressing a senator like that?"

He removed his leather jacket, then shrugged his shoulders underneath the cobalt USCP uniform. "I thought you were worth complimenting." His eyes were laser-focused on mine, but I had the impression he was imagining my body at that moment. It made me shiver with a strange mixture of annoyance and excitement.

The oven timer went off. I bent over in my silky pajamas to pull the dish out of the oven, and wondered if he was staring at my ass. I paused extra long before standing back up and closing the oven.

"Hope you like lasagna," I said.

"You kidding?" he replied. "My first name's Anthony. My mom's a second-generation Italian. Growing up, I ate lasagna as often as most kids drank water."

He did look vaguely Italian, now that I got a better look at him. That olive skin, the aquiline nose. I pulled out a serving spoon and pointed it at Anthony. "I know exactly why you made that comment to me on the Hill this afternoon."

"Because women like you should be told every single day how beautiful they are?" He began rolling up his sleeves, revealing those delicious tattoos. A dozen butterflies suddenly spun in my stomach. I fought them back down.

Get a grip, Elizabeth. You're 10 years his senior.

I narrowed my eyes at him. "You made that comment because you didn't know I was a senator. You thought I was an intern."

"Or a congressional aide." He burst out laughing and put up his hands in surrender. "But yeah, you got me. Forgive me for judging a book by its cover, but you're not like the other members of congress."

"Damn right I'm not," I said. He grinned like I'd made a dirty joke. I bent over the lasagna to cover my blush.

While I dished out the food, he helped himself to a glass from the cupboard and filled it with water like he was at home. Like everything else about this young motorcycle cop in my kitchen, the presumptuousness was simultaneously refreshing and annoying. Rather than sit at the table he took his plate standing up at the kitchen island, so I did the same on the other side.

He took a bite and moaned. The sound gave me the phantom twitch of a lady-boner. "Fucking hell, this is good."

"It's *my* mother's recipe," I said while blowing on a forkful of food. "She's not Italian, though."

"Could've fooled me." He took another bite,

ignoring that it was piping hot. "What's different? Something's different. I can tell."

I leaned forward on the counter. "If I told you, I'd have to kill you."

"Then I'll die happy."

"It's made with half ground beef, half ground sausage."

He chewed, staring off in thought. "This flavor's insane. Mom's gonna be furious when she finds out her lasagna's no longer my favorite."

"Then you'd better not tell her," I said. "Our little secret."

He grinned. "Our secret."

I poured another glass of wine, which almost finished the bottle. I was in that perfect place where I was buzzed, but not drunk. I would need to drink this last glass slowly to make sure I didn't have a hangover in the morning.

And to avoid making *other* mistakes.

I hadn't had a man like this in my apartment for a while. And never someone so *gorgeous*, not to mention flirty and forward. Was it just playful banter from someone killing time at the beginning of a long, cold shift? Or was he aiming for more?

I was the one who invited him inside. He could have stayed out there and none of this would have escalated. I'd be eating my lasagna alone watching reruns of Seinfeld on *Hulu*.

"Hey, what's this?" He picked up the birthday card.

"Don't," I said.

He grinned at the card. "I love these stupid cards. If a puppy says you're awesome, then you know it's true. Dogs can tell that sort of thing." He opened the card. "Oh shit. Was it your birthday recently?"

I raised my wine glass. "Today, actually. 35 years young."

He took a long look at me. "Damn, Senator O'Hare. I wouldn't have guessed you were older than 30."

"You're sweet." Then I added, "I was mostly joking about the Senator O'Hare stuff. You can call me Elizabeth."

"No way," he said, putting up a hand. The motion showed me more tattoos on the inside of his arm. "I don't want you reporting me for inappropriate behavior! You're Senator O'Hare from now on."

I smiled and took another bite of lasagna. It was a good batch tonight.

"Hey," he said as he set the birthday card down. "Now you can be president!"

I almost choked on my food. "What?"

"That's one of the requirements to be president," he said, like a third grader reciting facts from a textbook. "You have to be a natural born citizen, you cannot have already served two terms, and you have to be 35 years old." His dark eyes widened. "What's wrong?"

Shit. He didn't know anything—he was just making conversation. But now I was acting alarmed and suspicious...

"I never knew that," I said. I hoped I sounded nonchalant. "You only have to be 25 to be a congresswoman."

He gave me a funny look. "Seems like something a senator like you should know. Guess you've never thought about running from president then, huh?"

"Guess I haven't."

He looked at me longer. Studying me. Like he was going to figure it out...

"Hey." He looked around the kitchen. "Where's the birthday cake?"

"I didn't get one."

"No way. You've got to have cake on your birthday. How else are you going to blow out candles?"

There's something else I'd like to blow. The dirty thought came drifting across my mind, urged on by the wine. And although the thought started as a cheesy pun, it held an allure more delicious than any lasagna or cake.

"Want me to run out and get one?" Anthony asked. "I can get the bakery to write *Happy birthday, now you can be president!*"

"If you leave," I pointed out, "who's going to protect me from these imaginary bad guys intending me harm?"

"Easy solution: you hop on the bike and come with me. It's not every day I pick out birthday cake with one of the most powerful women in the country."

I chuckled. "I'm good, thanks."

"You ever ridden on a bike before?"

I imagined straddling his bike, my body pressed against his while the engine rumbled underneath us. My arms wrapped around his chest while we hugged the turns in the night...

"I have not," I said. "But I'm happy staying inside where it's warm, no matter how tempting cake is."

"I guess you have to be good at resisting temptation," he said casually. "When you're a politician, I mean."

"You have no idea."

He smiled like he knew exactly what I meant.

It felt wonderful to be flirty with a good-looking guy. Heck, it felt great just to look into an attractive man's eyes. No mask. Just two people being *real* together.

Even if it was just harmless flirting, it was nice.

It can be more than just flirting.

The thought purred in the back of my head. Anthony had already insinuated—as bluntly as possible—that he was attracted to me. And I sure as hell thought he was sexy. It wasn't an opinion. He *was* sexy. I felt the pull of him from across the kitchen island that separated us, like there was a lasso around my chest that he was pulling. I wanted nothing more than to give in to temptation, to throw him to the ground and mount him right here on the kitchen floor.

Soon, my life was going to irreversibly change. I would forever be under intense scrutiny, far more than any mere senator suffered. If I was going to do something, now was the time. Before Megan and I made our final decision.

I can't.

I knew I couldn't do it. Things had to be the way they were in the hotel room last night, masks and secrecy and then departing without so much as a goodbye kiss. I had too many aspirations to throw it all away for a night of passion.

Oh, but what a wonderful night of passion it would be.

Anthony's smile deepened as if he could read my mind. He stalked around the side of the kitchen island, reaching for me. But then his hand moved across me to grab the bottle of wine from the counter.

He took a swig straight from the bottle.

"Are you supposed to drink on the job?" I asked.

"There are rules," he admitted. "But a sip won't hurt. It'll help me stay awake to watch you all night."

Watch me all night. Touch me all night. Kiss me all night.

"Alcohol's a depressant," I pointed out.

He took another swig. "Not for me. It gets me all rowdy. Tell me something, Senator O'Hare. Why *didn't* you file a complaint against me today?"

"I'm a busy woman," I said. "If I reported every cocky guy who made an annoying comment I'd never get any real work done."

"Is that the only reason?" His smile deepened. He was leaning on the counter, so close to me I could practically feel the heat coming off his body. What did he look like underneath that crisp uniform?

"I also don't like punishing people for making dumb mistakes," I said. "Unless they're a political opponent I'm trying to crush."

He studied my face. Waiting for me to say more. "Wanna know what I think?"

"Not particularly, but you're going to tell me anyway, aren't you?"

He pointed the bottle at me and leaned in close. I had to tilt my head up to look into his eyes. "I think you didn't file a complaint because you *liked* it."

I sputtered a nervous laugh.

"Deep down, underneath all the layers you politicians put up, I think you *loved* being flirted with. I bet it made you feel like a real woman. Because you never let anyone close enough to make you feel that way. So when someone like me comes along and treats you the way a woman of your beauty *deserves* to be treated? Like someone sexy enough to peel the paint off the Capitol rotunda?" He took another swig of the wine. "It was the one thing you'd been craving. You can't file a complaint against someone who made you feel so *good*."

I was hardly breathing by the end. It was like he'd cracked open my head and was reading my thoughts back to me. In my world of politicians and lobbyists and sycophants, it was rare to talk to someone who spoke exactly what they were thinking without caring how blunt it sounded.

Anthony planted a hand on the counter and leaned toward me, a smug look spreading on his face. Waiting for me to admit he was right.

"Yes," I breathed. "Maybe I did want someone to appreciate me. A little bit."

He didn't gloat about being right. He only nodded.

I turned to face him directly.

Don't do it, Elizabeth.

"Now it's my turn to ask you a question," I said.

This is a mistake.

"And I want you to think very carefully before you answer."

"Yeah?" he asked.

You'll regret it later.

But I wanted it too badly to listen to the voice in my head.

"What do *you* want, Anthony?" I asked, voice soft and vulnerable. "What do you want, right now, at this moment in my kitchen while you look at me?"

He didn't take any time to think at all. A hungry smile tightened his beautiful face.

7

Elizabeth

Anthony's kiss was hard and forceful and tasted like sweet wine. One tattooed hand slipped around my neck and pulled me into him, against his warm body, and I felt every bit of him through my thin pajamas. His beard rubbed against my chin, smooth and then scratchy and *manly*, it had been so long since I'd kissed a man like this and it was what I needed more than anything.

I unbuttoned his shirt so he could shed it, and then he pulled his white undershirt up over his head. The tattoo on his neck ran down his chest into swirling tattoos of machine parts: gears, pistons, cannisters of steam. Interlaced in the machinery were roses, red ink among all the black.

I touched his chest, feeling the heat come off his skin. He began unbuckling his belt.

"You want to know what I want?" he answered in a deep, commanding voice. "*This* is what I want."

Anthony removed my pajama pants and then whirled me around. He bent behind me and dug his teeth into my ass cheek. Not painfully—just the right amount of pressure on the skin. The bite turned into a kiss as his fingers curled under the fabric of my panties, pulling them down. He took me immediately, just how I loved it. I bent over the counter and his cock was suddenly inside me, thick and hot and widening my inner walls in that wonderful ache of lust. I moaned loudly and looked back at him. He gazed back with pure desire in his eyes. The same look when he first saw me on the Hill today.

"Fucking *hell*," he moaned while gripping my waist. "You feel exactly how I imagined."

I closed my eyes as the Capitol Policeman fucked me from behind, a steady rocking from his hips. Faster and faster he went, our mutual moans echoing off the kitchen tile.

And as incredibly, tremendously, and *wonderfully* as it felt, I wanted something else.

I let him take me for a few more strokes before I twisted around to face him. I kissed him this time, forcing my tongue into his mouth to taste him some more. His own tongue writhed against mine wetly, making me wonder how it would feel against my clit.

I put my hands on the counter behind me and lifted myself up. Anthony grabbed my legs and held them in the air, then moved forward so that I could grip his cock and guide it inside.

Tonight I was going to look my lover in the eyes while he fucked me.

I touched myself with one hand, and ran my fingers over his tattooed chest with the other while he pumped me with his hard cock there on my kitchen counter. His eyes were dark pools filled with pleasure, intense pleasure for *me*, and it was better than a thousand nights with a stranger in a hotel.

It didn't take me long to climax, and when I did my orgasm was as intense as a white-hot sun, blinding me and blocking out all sound until I came down, trembling and panting.

Anthony grinned a feral grin. "Fucking hell, you're hot," he said.

I bit my lip as I watched him have his way with me. The veins in his pelvis bulged out against the bone. "This is better than birthday cake."

His fingers dug into my thighs as he gripped me tight. "This is better than most things."

His own groans of pleasure began rising, a steady warning siren of passion that I accepted with all my senses. This wasn't a man being paid to fuck me to completion. He was doing it because he *wanted* me. He needed it with as much immediacy and passion as I needed him.

When his deep moans reached their peak, I pushed him back and fell to my knees before him. I took the head of his cock in my mouth and stroked him while looking up at him through my eyelashes. His six-pack and muscular chest looked incredible from down here as he watched me suck him off, eyes growing wider with ecstasy.

"Oh *fuck*," he cried. "Senator O'Hare! *Elizabeth!*"

His jaw chewed at the air as he filled my mouth with his salty come. I took immense pleasure watching him enjoy it as rope after rope squirted into my mouth, his hips thrusting involuntarily with each one and his toes curling inside their socks.

I swallowed most of the load, but some still lingered on my tongue as I rose before him. I licked my lips to let him see it, then leaned in for a kiss. He didn't recoil or seem repulsed; if anything he enjoyed his own salty taste, his tongue rubbing against mine hungrily.

"Is that what you wanted?" I asked innocently.

He grinned. "Happy birthday, senator."

8

Elizabeth

"I bet you lied," I said.

We were sitting on my kitchen counter next to each other, passing a fresh bottle of wine back and forth. Anthony took the bottle and frowned at me.

"About being assigned to watch my house," I clarified. "That was just an excuse. You came here all on your own because you wanted to fuck a senator."

His laugh was rich and deep. "I can't say fucking a senator has ever been high on my list of things to do. But now?" He took a swig. "I've been missing out."

"I've never been with a cop before," I admitted. "So it's a night of firsts for both of us."

He touched my shoulder. "I didn't know you had ink too."

I twisted my arm around. "I've always loved butterflies. So carefree. Which is totally different than my own life. I bet that sounds silly."

"I think butterflies are cool."

"You're just saying that."

"I'm just saying that 'cause it's true." His finger ran down my arm, tracing the tattoos as he went. Finally he reached the flock of small birds on my wrist. "You don't usually see this sort of thing on a politician."

I laughed. "Tell me about it. I don't pretend like they're not there, but I usually wear long sleeves to cover them up. They severely limit my wardrobe in the summer."

"You could own it," he suggested. "Wear tank tops and let everyone see what you've got."

"If only. You'd be surprised how many polls show that people won't vote for someone with visible tattoos. A tattooed woman is right below *Muslims* and *atheists* on the list of things Ohioans are irrationally afraid of."

"Ever think of getting rid of them? Like, with lasers?"

"No," I answered immediately. "My campaign manager has suggested it, but I won't do it. They're part of me. Getting rid of them would be like getting rid of my fingers."

He nodded like he understood, and held out his own left arm. One tattoo was an inverse image of a heart: a splash of black ink on the outside with a perfect heart shape in the middle of untouched skin. Ornate designs like the back of a playing card ran up his hand, and were met by a hawk with its wings tucked into a dive. I grabbed his hand and brought it to my lips.

"We can't tell anyone about this," I whispered.

I didn't regret what had happened, but now I was beginning to worry about getting caught. What if one of his fellow officers came to relieve him, and found him inside rather than on his bike? What if someone else was watching my house and saw him *come* and go? What if Anthony, like most cocky men, wanted to brag about his conquests?

Anthony only barked a laugh.

"Of course we can't tell anyone," he agreed. "I'd get kicked off the force." He paused. "It'd probably be worse for you, right?"

I nodded. "This town loves a good sex scandal."

"Which is bullshit," Anthony said, fire suddenly in his voice. "You're not married. Who gives a shit if you have sex with someone?"

"I know!"

"If you were a bachelor," he said, "instead of a bachelorette, people would be cheering you on for getting some action. Instead, you're vilified. Fucking prudes."

"Preaching to the choir." I upended the bottle, then sighed. "You probably need to get back outside. Right?"

He shrugged. "There *is* that threat against your life."

"Those are always false alarms. We get hundreds of potential threats a day."

"Still, though..."

"It wasn't even against me," I added. "Apparently it was a vague threat against an unspecified female senator. That could be me, or one of the other 36 women in the senate."

Anthony hopped off the counter. "I like those odds."

I yelped as he threw me over his shoulder like a sack of senatorial potatoes. He was completely nude, giving me a perfect view of his chiseled ass. I gave it a hard smack as he carried me out of the kitchen, through the living room, and then up the stairs to my bedroom.

We made out on my bed for a while. Exploring each other's body with our hands. We weren't in a hurry. Eventually his hand found my wet pussy, and he was more tender than before as he rubbed me up and down. I moaned and stroked him in return.

Feeling adventurous, I rolled him over. His face was so pretty I couldn't bear it, so I straddled his head and lowered myself onto his face. His tongue penetrated deep inside of me while I rocked back and forth, his nose pressing into my clit. I could see the smile in his eyes as he wrapped his arms around my thighs and pulled me down into him. His tongue was a tornado on my insides, seemingly touching every nerve as I bucked and moaned and came all over his face.

I was still coming down when he threw me onto my back and fell between my legs. I was so wet from his mouth that his stiff rod slid right in. He wrapped his arms around me and held me close while making love with his entire body, staring deep into my eyes while enjoying every moment.

It could have lasted hours, or minutes. I couldn't tell. Everything in the world disappeared until it was just Anthony's muscular body pressed so tightly against mine I thought we'd fuse together, and when he came I kissed him so I could steal the breath from his lungs.

*

I lay in bed, staring at Anthony's sleeping body. I knew I should have regretted it, but I didn't. Not even a little bit.

There's a gorgeous man in my bed.

How long had it been? My last serious boyfriend was three years ago, when I was first campaigning for my senate seat. He couldn't handle the hectic schedule of the campaign, and I couldn't blame him. I hadn't dated anyone since then. It was tough to meet men when you were a public figure. And for all the fun I had with expensive male escorts in hotel rooms, I never actually *slept* with any of them.

Try as I might to enjoy the sight and feel and smell of Anthony, the risk crept up in the back of my head. There were hundreds of ways this could break bad. One stray photographer seeing him leave my apartment and all my political aspirations were toast. He seemed genuine about not telling anyone, but it was difficult to keep something like this *totally* secret. A few beers with the guys and it could slip out. Sure, he might leave the details vague. He'd tell them he slept with a *congresswoman*. But his buddies would start guessing names. Or maybe one of them would look at his past schedule and figure it out. Before long, the story would be sold to a tabloid and I'd have all the wrong kinds of publicity.

I curled up against his body. His leg was warm against mine, and the ink from his dark tattoos shone from the moonlight streaming through the window. It was easy to ignore the dangers when someone felt this *good*. This was turning out to be a fantastic birthday after all.

I closed my eyes and fell asleep, totally unaware that the false alarm security threat wasn't a false alarm at all.

9

Elizabeth

I woke when I usually did, five minutes before my alarm. Anthony was spooned against my back, the soft pressure of his semi-erection warm against my ass.

It was tempting to stay in bed. To have a little more fun. But I knew if I didn't go for my morning run I'd be cranky later. Besides, I had to burn off those red wine and lasagna calories.

I burned off plenty of calories last night.

I giggled and slipped out of bed, taking care not to wake Anthony. It wouldn't hurt to let him sleep until I got back. *Then* I would kick him out.

The freezing air smacked me in the face the moment I stepped outside. It had snowed during the night, a light dusting which immediately melted underneath my running shoes with each step. Certainly not enough snow to stop me from my workout.

I started my Garmin watch and took off down the dark street of my neighborhood.

I did my best thinking while jogging. There was something about the blood flow that really helped my mind wake up and immediately start churning. It helped me plan my day, preparing for long senate sessions and subcommittee interviews.

This morning, it helped me analyze what had happened last night.

Female politicians weren't allowed to have one-night stands. Men could do it as much as they wanted and they'd be compared to Bruce Wayne, but it made women look like sluts. Reckless, even. Anthony was right that it was bullshit, but that didn't make it any less true.

Anthony was wonderful. Exactly the kind of thing I needed before my entire life got turned upside-down with exploratory committees and campaign events and polling data. But although Anthony was the perfect kind of guy for a delicious fling, he was the poster child for what brought politicians down. He was a member of the United States Capitol Police. Not directly under my command, but vaguely subordinate. My political enemies could suggest I forced him to sleep with me. Especially considering I'd made specific threats about filing a report against him. Three other senators had been there on the Hill when it happened. If subpoenaed, they would testify that I *had* taken a picture of his badge and then threatened him.

Anthony would obviously say it was perfectly consensual without any overt or contextual threat, but it would all get dragged out into the public eye. The newspapers and network news stations would have a field day. Anthony's sexy, tattooed photo would be all over town with my name next to it.

Even though I couldn't stop picturing his nude body asleep in my bed right now, things were looking grim.

I pumped my arms and picked up speed as I rounded a corner. My blood was really flowing now.

Alright, so it had happened. Anthony and I fucked the shit out of each other last night. Now what?

Obviously I would need to sit him down and have a chat. A *real* talk, not just the 20 seconds of discussion we'd had before he threw me over his shoulder and carried me upstairs for round two. I needed to swear him to secrecy. Reiterate that both of our jobs were in jeopardy if word of this came out. Were non-disclosure agreements binding in this sort of situation? I didn't think so, but it wouldn't hurt to ask a lawyer. At the very least I could have Anthony sign a document verifying that the threats I made to his job were unrelated to our night together. It made me cringe to think of drafting up such a document and asking him to sign it, but sometimes a woman had to cover her ass.

Regardless of what I chose to do, one thing was certain: I wasn't going to tell Megan. After all the work she'd been doing on my potential campaign, she'd lose her mind to learn that I'd risked it all so carelessly.

Yet as important as secrecy obviously was, I felt ridiculously giddy by what had unfolded last night. I wanted to scream at the top of my lungs that there was presently a man in my bed, a man whose eyes I'd stared deeply into while we made love, and who I was tempted to go home and fuck one more time before I showered and went to the Hill.

I turned another corner, heading into the home stretch toward my apartment.

Sitting Anthony down this morning was the first step. Get some coffee in him and impress upon him the importance of secrecy. It would be an awkward conversation, but I thought he would understand.

A man stepped out of the alley ahead of me.

I didn't understand what he was doing at first. He was in the darkness between two street lights, with a hoodie covering his head and his hands in his pockets. He lingered on the sidewalk like he was lost, looking off to the right at nothing in particular. He was dressed too nice to be a bum, but I still considered crossing the street just to be safe.

Everything happened very quickly.

He turned toward me. His hand came out of his pocket gripping something heavy. He extended the object toward me. There was a bright flash, and a thunderclap so loud it hurt my ears from 50 feet away.

A gun.

I threw myself sideways into the street and scrambled on my hands and knees through the thin snow to take cover behind a parked car. Two more gunshots rang out, though it sounded—and felt—like my ears were full of cotton. The sound echoed off the surrounding buildings.

I'm being attacked.

I reached for my belt instinctively, then cursed. I'd forgotten to bring my taser and congressional alarm with me. I'd been too busy thinking about the hot man in my bed.

I'm totally, completely, vulnerable.

I could hear the man's shoes squeaking through the snow as he drew closer. "Hey," he called in a raspy voice. "Come out so we can make this quick."

Huddled there on the ground in my running clothes, fear paralyzed me.

I forced myself to peek up above the car. I could see him through the car windows. He was coming closer, but reluctantly. Maybe he thought I might have a gun too.

"Come any closer and I'll shoot!" I yelled in a shaky voice.

His laugh was bitter. "You don't got nothin'."

Sheer terror gripped my lungs, making it impossible to breathe. I was a sitting duck if I made a run for it. But the closer he came, the less likely he was to miss.

I made a decision: I needed to run. I had to do it *now*, before he got any closer. I knew this fact intellectually but my body wouldn't cooperate.

And then, with horrifying clarity, I realized: *I'm going to die.*

"All I want..." the man said as he came around the side of the car.

A deep voice called out: "Capitol Police! Put your hands where I can see them!"

Gunshots thundered farther up the street. My attacker cursed, then began running. Two more gunshots split the air, followed by a cry of pain.

Unable to do anything else, I trembled against the car.

Anthony appeared moments later. He was wearing only his boxers and a tank top over his tan, tattooed skin. Not caring about his bare feet or knees, he immediately dropped down next to me.

"Shh, it's okay," he whispered, wrapping an arm around me. "I'm here, Elizabeth. You're safe now."

He whispered soothing words into my ear while carrying me back inside.

10

Elizabeth

I sat at my kitchen table, cradling a mug of coffee in both hands. I still wore my running clothes. Even though we were inside my warm apartment, I was starting to get cold. The shock and adrenaline wearing off, probably.

"Ma'am?" said one of the officers seated across from me. He looked like he was 80, though his eyes were hardened with experience. The other officer was closer to my age, and tapped her pen against her notepad while waiting for my answer.

I shook my head. "Sorry. I couldn't see his face. He was wearing a hoodie."

"What about his hair?" the older officer asked. "Long, short, dark, light?"

"I don't know."

"Anything you can tell us will be immensely valuable."

"I don't know."

"Ma'am..."

"She said she doesn't know," Anthony snapped. He was leaning against the wall a respectable distance away. Fully clothed in his uniform and jacket. "Ease off her."

The older officer, who outranked Anthony, twisted in his chair and stared him down. Anthony crossed his arms and shifted his weight from one leg to the other. He seemed worried about the attack. Worried about *me*.

"What happened next?" the younger officer asked. "After he stepped out from the alley?"

I told them everything that happened. There wasn't much to tell. The younger officer took far more notes than my explanation warranted.

"There aren't many muggings in this neighborhood," the older officer said, "but it's not unheard of."

"Mugging," I repeated.

"Huh?"

"Well," I said, "for a mugger he didn't seem interested in my belongings. He just appeared and started firing."

"Tweakers," the younger officer said. "Guys so high they can't think logically. That's all."

"Tweakers," I repeated.

"Can you go over what he said to you again? Word for word?"

I spent a few moments describing the assailant's raspy voice.

"How much time elapsed before Officer duBois returned fire on the suspect?"

I shrugged. "30 seconds? Maybe more. I can't remember. I was busy being shot at."

The officer twisted in his seat again. "Officer duBois? You wanna join us?"

"I'm fine right here."

I couldn't see the older officer's face, but I could hear the ice in his words. "If you were stationed outside her house on your bike, why did it take you so long to respond?"

Oh crap. That's why Anthony was worried: because he was sleeping in my bed when the attack happened. He was supposed to be outside my apartment.

"Maybe it was only a few seconds," I quickly added. The younger officer looked sharply at me. "It was tough to tell in the heat of the moment. Everything happened so fast, you know?"

Anthony took a slow, deep breath. "I responded as quickly as I could," he said through gritted teeth. "Gunshots rang out. I drew my sidearm and approached on foot. As soon as the suspect was in sight I commanded him to put his hands in the air. He turned toward me, which is when I saw he had a weapon in his hand. Then I opened fire."

The younger officer cleared her throat. "Did you see Senator O'Hare leave her apartment?"

Anthony hesitated. "I saw *someone* leave her apartment. From my bike I couldn't tell if it was the senator or not."

"And you didn't offer to escort her?" she asked. "You remained at your post even though the target of the threat had left the building?"

"My orders were to watch the apartment," Anthony said. I could tell he was done with all this. "So I watched the apartment. I shot the guy in the leg, by the way. He shouldn't be hard to find; just follow the fucking blood. Then *he* will tell you how quickly I was on his ass."

"There's no need for your tone," the older officer said.

"Fuck my tone. You two are more concerned about how long it took me to respond than the fact that someone just tried to kill Elizabeth."

There was an uncomfortable silence. Both officers stared at Anthony.

"Senator O'Hare," he corrected after too long of a pause. "Someone tried to kill Senator O'Hare, and you two are focusing on the wrong thing. Why aren't you out there collecting the asshole's blood?"

"We have a forensics team outside collecting evidence," the officer calmly said.

Anthony blinked. "Good."

There was a noise out in my hall. A police officer arguing with a woman. Moments later Megan came striding into my kitchen. "What the heck is going on outside?" she demanded. The crazed look in her eyes didn't disappear until she saw me.

"What are you doing here?" I asked.

"Since our meeting yesterday got interrupted, I figured I would try to catch you after your morning run." She hefted the folder she'd shown me yesterday. "Elizabeth, what happened?"

"Senator O'Hare was attacked," the older officer said.

Megan's eyes widened. "Elizabeth!" she came running over to where I sat at the table. I let her hug me.

"Senator," the younger officer said. "Do you know of anyone who would want to cause you harm?"

I couldn't help but laugh. "I'm a senator from a

swing state. Half my constituents hate me. Not to mention half the people in *this* town."

Megan took the question more seriously. "We get death threats every day, officer. I'll have the most recent ones forwarded to your office."

"That would be helpful."

I spun my head to face Megan. "Every day? Seriously?"

Her face was grim. "Just about, yeah. Most are nutjobs who don't pose any real threat. Assholes venting on the internet."

"And you're just now telling me this?"

"Every politician gets some number of death threats," she said simply. "There's no point in concerning you unless they pose an immediate risk. You already have too much on your mind."

I knew she was right, but it still annoyed me to be left in the dark. Every single day?

"Are you done with her?" Megan asked. The police said they were, and Megan turned to me. "I'll meet you for lunch on the Hill so we can talk about this."

She led the police officers out of my apartment while telling them it was crucial to keep this attack from leaking to the press, insisting the timing was politically sensitive. I shook my head. She hadn't asked *who* attacked me, or how, or even if I was alright. She went straight to thinking about how it would affect the campaign.

Granted, that's what I paid her for.

Anthony lingered in my kitchen, his eyes focused on me. "You okay, sugar?"

"I'm still shaken up," I admitted. I stood, and my legs felt weak. "I've never had a gun pointed at me before."

Anthony came over and embraced me. This time I accepted it gratefully. I melted into his warm arms just like I'd melted into them last night, but totally different at the same time. He made me feel safe. Within seconds I wasn't afraid anymore.

"I'm sorry," he whispered into my hair. "I should have been outside on my bike..."

I squinted up at him. "Shut up. You're being stupid."

"It's my fault."

"*Really* stupid." I bopped him on the nose. "If not for you, I'd be dead."

"We can't tell them anything," he said, cupping my chin with his tattooed hand. "Last night was amazing, Elizabeth. But now, with this attack? They'll have my head for abandoning my post."

"It would be disastrous for both of us," I agreed. He seemed to understand the severity of the situation. Heck, now *he* was in a worse position than *me*. A senator was attacked because he shirked his duty.

"I'm glad you left your post," I said, putting a hand on his uniformed chest.

I could tell he wanted to stay. His grip on my body was passionate and needful, holding my hips against his. I didn't want him to leave either.

But then he quickly looked around and pulled away as if remembering we might be seen together. "I've got to go."

He turned away, but I grabbed his arm to stop him.

"Thank you, Anthony," I said. "For saving my life."

A small smile touched his lips. "Just doing my job, Senator O'Hare."

And just like that, he was gone.

11

Elizabeth

It was hard to focus on the Hill. I kept re-living the end of my jog everywhere I went. In the senate chambers, in the office hallway, even in the women's bathroom I kept imagining a hooded figure appearing ahead of me. Drawing a gun. Aiming it at my chest.

A few of the other senators on the finance committee knew something had happened. Word traveled fast in this town. I brushed it off as a potential mugging. A totally random event.

Even though I feared it was anything but.

The morning was a blur. I was in my own head throughout the morning senate session, and I might as well have been a mannequin for all the talking I did on my subcommittees.

"Senator O'Hare," said Bob Pollock, the senator from Florida, catching up to me in the hallway after the committee.

"Senator Pollock. I'm surprised to see you on the Hill and not out on the campaign trail." He'd announced his candidacy for president two weeks prior.

He smiled a politician's smile at me. "Still plenty of work to do here before I start courting Iowa and New Hampshire. Can't let a campaign get in the way of what the people of Florida elected me to do."

"A noble viewpoint," I said. "How can I help you?"

He stopped me there in the hall, then looked both ways to make sure nobody was within earshot. His tan face was filled with concern. "I heard about what happened this morning."

I groaned. "You and everyone else on the Hill."

"I'm not going to bother you about it," he said. "I just wanted to say that I hope this doesn't discourage you from any future political aspirations. You're one of the most compelling young senators in our party. Our country would lose something special if you let an attack like this scare you away from public service."

The words were as encouraging as they were unnecessary. "It was just a mugging gone wrong."

"Sure it was," he said.

"But I appreciate the kind words. It's going to take more than 30 seconds of harassment to steer me away from politics."

That politician's smile touched his lips again. "I'm overjoyed to hear it."

I grabbed food from the cafeteria and carried it back to my office. Megan was waiting inside. I handed her a salad and then tore open the container holding my cheeseburger. Megan raised an eyebrow at my food.

"No salad today?" she asked.

"Someone tried to kill me this morning," I said. "One cheeseburger isn't going to hurt."

"Speaking of this morning," Megan began.

I cut her off with a gesture. "Please no. The last thing I want to talk about is the mugging. Everyone, including Senator Pollock, has been whispering about it."

Her eyebrows climbed up her forehead. "Bob Pollock talked to you? What did he say?"

"Enough, Megan. Let's go over that folder of yours."

Megan pulled it out of her bag and tossed it on my desk. The opposition research we'd ordered.

"Well?" I asked, afraid to touch it.

Megan took a bite of salad and grinned. "You're clean. You passed."

I breathed a sigh of relief and opened the folder, sifting through it while she talked.

"They found some tame stuff from high school. There's video recording of you arguing an anti-Israel stance while on the debate team, but obviously that's only because you drew that stance at competition and not because you legitimately hold that belief. You smoked weed in college, but thankfully nobody cares about that anymore. Honestly, the worst thing on your entire record is the plagiarism accusation in college."

I grimaced. "I figured they'd dig that up. It was totally unintentional. A single paragraph in a 40 page essay on Hamilton's Federalist Papers."

"You were put on academic probation for a semester," Megan said. "Which looks bad, but at least you weren't expelled. That won't play well with certain demographics but it's not terrible in the grand scheme of things." She pointed her salad fork at me. "That's more or less it. There are no serious roadblocks."

I grinned. What she was saying was beginning to sink in.

"How about it, Elizabeth?" Megan asked. "You ready to announce your candidacy?"

I'd wanted to become President of the United States since I was a little girl, when we went on a family trip to Washington. I was only 12, but I knew it then with certainty. No other aspiration would suffice.

But a woman had to work her way up in

politics. I got my degree in political science and ran for city council back home in Ohio. I ran circles around the small town politicians and quickly rose to state senate. From there it was easy to jump into the race for Ohio District Five, where I served two terms before unseating Senator Kopeck for his senate seat.

I loved civil service. It was fulfilling working on things that *mattered*, knowing I was helping people back home. I woke up every single day excited to go to work on the Hill and try to make our country a better place.

But throughout all those years, I kept my sights laser-focused on what I *really* wanted.

Now my chance was here. I was 35 and eligible to run for president. I grinned back at my campaign manager.

"Let's run for vice president!"

I wasn't naive. I knew my chances of winning a presidential primary were slim to none. I looked too young, I had too little experience, and I was single. That was a surprisingly strong turnoff for a lot of voters. People wanted a politician with a spouse and family. That was true for male politicians, but it was *especially* true for women.

That was okay. Our goal wasn't to win the presidency just yet. Our goal was to make a splash in the primary and get picked as the VP for whichever candidate *did* win the primary. Because I had something incredibly valuable.

18 electoral votes.

Ohio was a swing state. And despite this morning's attack, my approval rating among Ohioans was high. Picking me as VP would all but guarantee a candidate the state of Ohio, and likely the election overall. Hopefully that person would be Senator Bob Pollock. So far, he was the strongest candidate in the field by a wide margin. And if he carried his home state of Florida in the general election? We couldn't lose.

If everything worked out the way I hoped, eight years as vice president would help me build experience and name recognition with the American people. By then I would be 43, the same age Kennedy won the 1960 election.

Megan and I had carefully crafted the plan for years, waiting for the right moment. Now that I'd passed a thorough background check from a skilled opposition researcher, there were no more roadblocks in our way.

"When should we announce?" I asked as I bit into my cheeseburger.

There was so much work to do. A presidential campaign required an enormous staff and boatloads of money, not to mention carving time out of my already slammed senate schedule. It would be weeks before we were ready to announce.

But Megan surprised me by saying, "This weekend."

I almost choked on my food. "What! So soon?"

"Yes! We're going to take advantage of this morning's assassination attempt."

"Please don't use the A-word," I said. "It was a mugging."

She gave me a patient look. "Muggers usually, you know, *mug* someone. The police told me he shot first?"

"He was probably a tweaker."

"A sitting senator getting shot at is not a coincidence, Elizabeth. You may want to avoid that fact, but as your campaign manager I can't. I want to use it to our advantage. Gain some sympathy support. Make you look strong."

"We're not using this as a political crutch," I insisted. "I'm serious, Megan."

She chewed her bite of salad, swallowed, and looked back at me coolly. "What did I tell you when you first hired me?"

"You said you would do *anything* to win."

"That's right. *Anything*, no matter how much you don't like it. You're about to launch the biggest campaign of your career. I can't ignore a political opportunity like this. I'm going to kick the tires with my pollsters and see how this morning's attack will play, but I already know the answer. It'll give you more media attention than we ever could've dreamed. Here's what I'm envisioning. We find an excuse to go back to

Columbus for the weekend. I can schedule an event. Then we get the Capitol Police to release information about the attack. An assassination attempt is a big deal. It'll be on every news station. That's when you give a public statement. We'll have you talk about not letting fear get in the way of your dreams, or in the way of greatness. I can see the speech in my head already. You'll crush it."

I wanted to protest more, but Megan was like a dog chasing a tennis ball. There was no stopping her once she set her mind to something. Plus, I had to admit it was a cunning way of announcing my candidacy for president. I would have to make a statement about the attack this morning regardless, so why not combine the two?

"Alright," I said. "There may be something to that."

She gave a single emphatic nod. "Now that's out of the way, I do want to bump up your security. I've hired a private bodyguard for you."

I groaned.

"He starts tonight."

"Come on, Megan..."

"Someone tried to assassinate you this morning. This is serious, Elizabeth! Why aren't you taking it seriously?"

"I have the Capitol Police watching my house," I said. Images of Anthony nude in my bed bombarded me. The delicious tattoos on his chest and neck and arm...

Megan rolled her eyes. "I'm not impressed with them. That bad boy with the tattoos didn't respond very quickly. You need someone by your side."

"I can't have a bodyguard tailing me all around the Hill," I said. "He'll get in the way."

"Senator Kirono has had a bodyguard with her for three years," Megan pointed out.

I scoffed. "That big dude with a head like a bowling ball? He's in the way *constantly*. I don't want another one of them."

"The bodyguard I hired comes highly recommended," Megan replied. "You won't get added to anyone's presidential ticket if you're dead."

"That's not true," I said. "Dead people have won elections before."

"I'm serious, Elizabeth."

I took another bite out of my cheeseburger. All this talk about assassination attempts and potential death was diminishing my appetite.

"This is too much right now. I'm still rattled from this morning. Can we please focus on the campaign itself?" I asked. "The part that actually matters?"

We went over campaign data for the rest of lunch. Polling on specific issues and ways to stand out as a candidate. Minutia such as the best time of day to make the announcement, and the best venue. Even data on whether to wear a pencil skirt or pantsuit for the announcement. We settled on the Ohio Statehouse in Columbus, where I first ran for city council.

"So that's it," I said as I packed up to return to the senate chamber. "We're really going to do this?"

"We really are."

I couldn't get rid of the silly smile on my face. Megan was just as giddy. We were like schoolgirls who knew the Prom King was going to ask us to dance.

"I'll get the ball rolling on everything," she said. "Try to go about your day as if nothing's different."

"I'll do my best," I said doubtfully. It was going to be tough listening to old senators ramble about bill riders this afternoon.

Megan's phone rang as I was leaving. "Wait, what?" She snapped her fingers to get my attention and gestured for me to wait. "Is this a joke? Who decided that? Well, go find out! Senator O'Hare doesn't have time for this petty nonsense."

"What is it?" I asked.

She covered the receiver. "If you didn't like my bodyguard idea, you're *really* going to hate this."

12

Luca

It was 12:05 on a Tuesday afternoon when I got the most ridiculous assignment of my life.

Agent Frank Blixen, my boss, tossed a folder across his desk. "There was an attack on a senator's life this morning." He leaned back in his chair behind his desk as if that was all that needed to be said. "That's your new assignment."

"A *senator?*" I asked.

"You heard me, Agent Santos."

I didn't touch the folder. That would be akin to acceptance. And I wasn't going to accept anything about this.

"Elizabeth O'Hare, from Ohio," Agent Blixen said, as if that helped. "Man with a gun opened fire on her during her morning jog."

"None of that answers my question," I growled.

"You didn't ask a question. You're just sitting there, sulking."

"Why is a senator getting a Secret Service detail?" I asked. "And why in the fuck is it getting dumped on me?"

Frank got up and closed the door to his office. The blinds on the window rattled against the glass. He sat back down, crossed his arms, and said in a sympathetic voice, "I think you know the answer to the second question, Luca."

Because I fucked up last week.

I was near the end of my shift in the West Wing when I was sent to relieve another agent near the Roosevelt room. I knocked before entering, but the senior member of the cabinet inside the room hadn't heard me. Neither had the young intern with whom he was vigorously engaged in... *activity*. I'd immediately apologized and left the room, and when they both came out moments later the cabinet member only nodded politely at me. But I could tell by the look in his eyes that I'd fucked up.

And now I was being punished.

"The Secret Service doesn't give protection to senators," I said stubbornly. "Not unless they're running for president and have already won their primary."

"Protection is authorized at the sole discretion of the DHS Secretary," Agent Blixen said. "This detail is unusual, but it is not unprecedented."

I gave in and opened the file. A photograph was on top of the stack of information. Elizabeth O'Hare was young and very pretty, with a sharp wit shining in those almond eyes. My first reaction was vaguely sexist: why would anyone want to hurt a pretty little thing like her?

Of course, she was a senator. I buried my prejudices deep down and forced myself to look at her as a target requiring protection.

"She's in the opposition party to the administration," I said.

"So what?"

"I could understand offering a scared senator a Secret Service detail if they were a member of the same party. As a favor. But someone across the aisle? Why's the DHS Secretary putting this out there?"

Agent Blixen stared at me for a long moment. "I can't confirm this, but supposedly this is coming from POTUS himself."

POTUS. The phonetic nickname for President Of The United States.

"Then my question is even more relevant. Why extend this courtesy to a member of the opposition party?"

"It's not our job to question why. It's our job to protect." He tapped the photo. "And you've been chosen to protect Senator O'Hare. All the details are inside."

"There's got to be something you can do," I pleaded.

"What I can do is tell you to stop complaining and do your job," he snapped.

"Or maybe I'll just quit."

He laughed mockingly. "Luca, you've been doing this too long to throw a tantrum and quit."

"I've been doing this too long to deserve this shit."

"I don't disagree."

"Then help me fight this!" I exclaimed. "Push back. Give the assignment to a rookie. There are plenty of them who wouldn't mind following a junior senator around like a puppy."

Agent Blixen only shook his head. "Listen. You're smart, so I'm going to level with you. You pissed off the wrong people, and now you're in the shithouse. Yeah, it sucks. Yeah, you probably don't deserve it. But you want to get back in the administration's good graces? Here's your chance. Senator O'Hare was almost assassinated this morning on her morning jog. The attacker got away. Follow her, protect her, keep her safe. That's your assignment, Agent Santos."

I stood and snatched the folder off his desk. "Yes, sir."

I stomped down the hall of the U.S. Secret Service Headquarters. I must have had a look on my face because nobody called out to me or asked me what was wrong. Everyone gave me a wide berth.

I'd been a special agent for 15 years now. I'd protected three different presidents and their families. I'd traveled the world as part of their detail, always on alert for even the smallest potential threat. I'd served my country in a way that made me proud.

This assignment was a slap in the face to everything I had done.

I had always been good at controlling my emotions. The trick was not to fight it. To allow yourself a moment of weakness so that it was all out of your system, leaving only hardened resolve behind.

So as I stormed out of the headquarters, I glanced at my watch. I would allow myself five minutes to be bitter and upset. Five minutes to be angry at the people who had done this to me: the senior cabinet member who was careless enough to fool around with an intern in the Roosevelt room; the POTUS who agreed to allow such a ridiculous assignment; the bosses in the Secret Service who didn't push back on the request.

By the time five minutes was over, I was walking down the street feeling much better.

I took a deep breath and changed my entire mentality. Like Agent Blixen had said, this was my chance to get back in the administration's good graces. Senator O'Hare had almost been killed this morning, and according to the information in the folder the threat was still high. She was young and very smart. She had a bright career ahead of her.

So long as I kept her safe.

Being a special agent in the Secret Service meant protecting some of the most important people in our nation. A senator was not that far below the POTUS. More powerful, in some ways. This was an assignment I would take as seriously as possible.

I rounded a corner and the beautiful Capitol rotunda came into view two blocks ahead. I would protect Senator O'Hare. I would die to keep her safe if that's what it took.

Even if this whole thing was bullshit.

13

Elizabeth

"This whole thing is *bullshit*," Megan grumbled.

"I don't understand," I said as we walked through the Capitol Building. "I thought the Secret Service only protected the president and his family."

"That's why this is bullshit," Megan replied. "POTUS must know you're planning on running. So he's assigning you a Secret Service detail to make you look weak, like you need protecting. Undercutting our entire message before the campaign starts."

I groaned.

"The good news is you don't need a private

bodyguard anymore," she grumbled. "He was supposed to be at your apartment tonight, but I'll call and cancel." She stopped at the entrance and faced me. "Don't let this distract you. POTUS may be undercutting our campaign already, but he can't silence our message. We'll crush it when we announce this weekend."

"Right."

The special agent was waiting when I got back to my subcommittee. He wore the standard black suit and tie, with an American flag pin over his heart. He had short, sandy hair that might have had a few grey hairs mixed in, but it was tough to tell. His face was experienced, and he was a little older than me—maybe 40. He had a rugged handsomeness about him, but he was too grizzled and serious.

He stood very still and looked all around with his eyes, almost ignoring me as I approached. "Senator O'Hare," he said. A statement, not a question.

"I don't need Secret Service protection," I said. "But I'm guessing it's not up to you, is it?"

"No, ma'am."

"Please don't call me ma'am. I think I'm younger than you."

"Probably, ma'am."

"Seriously." I extended my hand. "Elizabeth."

He shook my hand and finally met my gaze. His cobalt eyes were sharp and searching. I got the impression he didn't miss much.

"Special agent Luca Santos," he said. "Where to next, Elizabeth?"

I gave a start. "Aren't you supposed to know?"

"I've reviewed your file, but your full schedule has not yet been sent to my office. Tomorrow I'll be clearing all areas prior to your arrival."

"Fantastic," I muttered.

By himself, he wasn't annoying. He went into committee rooms ahead of me and checked my chair before I entered and sat down, then he took up a spot on the wall behind me. What *was* annoying was the attention it generated. I was like the kid who got to bring her puppy to school. It captured everyone's attention and made it difficult to get anything done.

The afternoon session in the senate chamber was especially cumbersome. Luca followed me as I walked around and spoke with my senate colleagues. Some senators from the opposing party outright laughed when they saw him. Several more whispered to each other, and one loudly exclaimed, "I thought candidates didn't get a Secret Service detail until they won the primary."

I ignored him, but it took a lot of willpower. If there had been rumors about my possible candidacy before, soon it would be an open secret. By the time I *did* make the announcement, my candidacy would be old news.

Megan and I went out to dinner that evening to discuss the campaign some more. Luca tailed us in his own car and followed us into the restaurant. We had a reservation for two, and the restaurant was too full to accommodate anyone else, but Luca flashed his badge and a separate table was quickly prepared for him.

That's how we had dinner: Megan and I chatting softly while a special agent watched like a stalker from two tables over. At least he didn't insist on taste-testing my food for me.

Megan and I hugged outside the restaurant when we were done. "Have a good night. And maybe skip your jog in the morning?"

I snorted. "Shouldn't you be telling me that the best thing to do politically is to put on a strong face? Go about my day as if nothing happened?"

"That may be true... But I do worry about *you*, Elizabeth. Not just your candidacy."

I gave her a strong smile. "I'm not letting one nutjob ruin my daily routine. Besides," I added, "I have Agent Santos here to protect me."

He nodded. "Yes ma'am."

Luca was lockstep beside me as we walked to the cars, his head swiveling around, scanning for threats.

"I told you not to call me ma'am."

"Force of habit."

"Then I'm calling you Luca," I said. "Maybe

that will help you be less formal."

"Whatever you say, Elizabeth." We reached the cars and he held out his hand. "Keys."

"Excuse me?"

"From now on, I'm driving you wherever you need to go. In case we are attacked in transit and I need to make a swift getaway."

"You've got to be kidding."

His face was hard and serious.

I sighed and handed over my keys. Maybe it wouldn't be so annoying if I pretended he was a private chauffeur.

He left his car in the parking lot as we got into mine and drove away.

It was strange being in the passenger seat of my own car. It was strange suddenly getting all this security attention. It was strange having a man try to kill me.

Was this a taste of what running for president would be like? It was enough to make me doubt my path forward.

"So," I said to distract myself. "Any leads on the guy who tried to kill me?"

His face remained blank, but his fingers tightened on the wheel. "Very few. They expedited the blood work collected from the scene, but there were no matches in the criminal database. And the only bullets recovered were from the officer who returned fire. They can't find any from the attacker."

"Is that unusual?"

He shrugged one shoulder. "Might be unusual. Might just mean the USCP did a lazy job searching the surrounding area."

"Hmm," I said, thinking about that. "So how's tonight going to work? Do you stand at the foot of my bed and watch me sleep?"

"I'm only covering you during the day," Luca said. The alternating streetlights sent shadows running over his hard jawline in the darkness. "We're working in conjunction with the USCP. The Capitol Police will continue watching your house at night."

Anthony. The thought of him outside my apartment right now filled me with excitement. The first *real* lover I'd had in ages.

I'm about to begin my campaign. Last night was fun, but it was a one-time thing.

I still looked forward to seeing him the entire drive home.

But when we arrived, it was a police cruiser parked outside my apartment, not a motorcycle. And neither of the officers who stepped out of it were Anthony.

"Ma'am," said the same officer who'd been taking notes last night. Her breath fogged in front of her face. "My partner and I will be watching the house all night."

I resisted the urge to ask where Anthony was. "Alright."

I grabbed my bag from the car and went up the steps to my porch. Both Luca and the officer followed.

"What are you doing?" I asked her.

She jerked her head over her shoulder. "One in the cruiser, one on the door. Not taking any chances this time."

"Of course," I grumbled. Then, after collecting myself, I said, "Sorry if I seem unappreciative. It's been a long day. Thank you for protecting me."

"Don't think anything of it, ma'am. You expecting anyone tonight?"

A wave of panic gripped me until I realized she was asking for *professional* reasons. "No, nobody. I'm probably going right to bed."

I glanced at Luca, who was still lingering too. "You waiting for a goodnight kiss?"

The officer snickered.

Luca was unamused. "I want to check your apartment before I leave for the night."

I gritted my teeth, but didn't resist.

Luca stalked around my apartment with slow, careful steps. As if an attacker would leap out at any moment. He reminded me of an adult checking all the closets for the boogieman to make a child feel safe. I didn't like that *I* was the child in this scenario. I followed him as he made his rounds through the apartment and tried not to seem annoyed by his intrusiveness.

My bedsheets were still tangled from last night's activity. I tensed, but Luca didn't seem to even notice. He went into the bathroom, then checked the locks on all the windows. Finally he nodded as if he was satisfied.

"Everything looks secure." He handed me a card. "Call me if you need anything. I'll be waiting in the morning. Have a good night, Elizabeth."

I smiled, grateful that he hadn't called me ma'am. "You too, Luca."

When he was gone I locked my front door and engaged the deadbolt. Maybe I was overanalyzing things, but I got the impression Luca didn't like being on my detail. Like it was a shitty assignment for someone in his position.

But as silly as it sounded, having him check my house *did* make me feel safer. That and the officers outside. I could see her silhouette through the windows next to my front door. Just standing there.

I wish it was Anthony instead.

I could almost feel his presence in the house. Like the smell of him still lingered on the furniture and carpet. I took a deep breath and sighed, the memories from last night still fresh in my mind.

And he'd saved my life this morning. He shot my attacker, and then carried me inside where I was safe. I felt closer to him, somehow. Like we shared a special bond.

Thank goodness they had sent two other officers. The temptation of having him here would have been too great.

Why *hadn't* they sent him back tonight? Had he gotten in trouble for not responding quickly enough? Was it just a normal rotation of officers? I was almost tempted to ask the officer on my front porch. Or to call the station and request him personally. Senators did that all the time with Capitol Police they were familiar with on the Hill. It wouldn't be unusual.

It would be extremely obvious. Stop acting stupid.

"What has gotten into you, Elizabeth?" I muttered to myself.

I changed out of my work suit and into a soft robe, then went into the kitchen. I ate a yogurt and stared at the counter where I'd been sitting about 24 hours ago, legs spread wide while Anthony worked me up and down. I couldn't stop thinking about it. I couldn't stop thinking about *him*.

My doorbell rang.

I went to the entrance hall. Two shapes were on the other side of the glass. One was the taller, wider shape of a man.

The second officer, probably. But what my brain thought was: *Anthony! Maybe it's Anthony!*

When I opened the door, I was faced with the *last* man I ever expected to see outside my apartment.

14

Elizabeth

He was tall and beautiful. He wore jeans and a black leather jacket, with a tight t-shirt underneath that clung to his powerful muscles. He had wavy blond hair like a surfer, a perfectly smooth face, and a nose and smile that reminded me of Owen Wilson.

He was a devastatingly handsome man.

The kind of man you would pick out of a digital catalog to meet you in a hotel room.

Ethan.

"What are *you* doing here?" I blurted out, like an idiot.

The officer frowned. "He says you're expecting him, but you told me you weren't having anyone else over..."

Behind her, the other officer was outside of his cruiser and speaking into his radio.

Pure fear smashed into my psyche. Ethan, the escort I'd been sleeping with, had learned who I was. He'd found me. He was here to blackmail me, to demand money or political favors or something worse. My candidacy was over before it had even started.

Ethan patted the air in a calming gesture. "Everyone relax. I was hired by your campaign manager, Megan Hanram. I'm from Silver Springs Security. I'm your bodyguard, Senator O'Hare."

The relief almost knocked me to my knees. It was quickly replaced by suspicion. What were the odds that the escort I'd been hiring also happened to be a bodyguard by day?

And one assigned to me?

He didn't seem to recognize me from the hotel, though. Or else he hid it well. But how long until he found out? He always saw me nude, or wearing only lingerie. I always wore a mask with him. The tattoos on my arm would give me away, but my robe sleeves covered them right now.

A more immediate thought came to mind: why was he here? Megan was supposed to call them to cancel.

"I don't need a bodyguard," I said.

"Ms. Hanram said you would protest," he said with a laugh. It was the same rich laugh he made in the hotel room when deciding how he was going to take me. Right before pinning me to the bed with his weight. Smothering me with his muscular body, wrapping an arm around my chest and holding me close while whispering dirty ideas into my ear...

I waved a hand. "No, I'm—it's not that. We don't need a bodyguard anymore because I've been assigned a Secret Service detail."

"Secret Service agents don't protect senators." He stared at me with piercing green eyes. It felt incredible to actually stare into them without a mask separating us. Eyes like an Irish meadow. A girl could lay down and fall asleep in those eyes.

The officer rescued me from my dreamy daze. "We're working in conjunction with the Service. Her detail left 10 minutes ago."

Now Ethan looked *really* confused. He eyed me up and down as if wondering what was so special about me. "Ms. Hanram insisted I don't take no for an answer. She said you were stubborn."

I could have told him to leave. I *didn't* need him now that I had Luca protecting me during the day. The Capitol Policewoman was staring at me, waiting for the word to kick him off my porch.

But now that Ethan, the man I'd been sleeping

with for over a month in secret, was here in front of me? Staring into my own eyes without the hindrance of a mask? I didn't have it in me to say no.

"Nice to meet you," I said. I started to offer him my hand but stopped when I remembered the tattoos he would see. "Call me Elizabeth."

"I'm Ethan."

So that is his real name. Or he used a fake name for both jobs.

I nodded to the police officer and then let him inside.

We lingered in the entrance hall. My brain was screaming at me: *the escort you've been hiring is here in your apartment.*

He smelled enticingly familiar, a soft lavender and vanilla cologne. Would he be able to smell me too? I usually wore perfume when we got together, but I never did while I was on the Hill.

"The contract Ms. Hanram sent me was very specific, so let me go over the ground rules," he said. "I'm still waiting on my clearance, so I can't follow you around inside the Capitol Building itself. But I'll be covering you the rest of the day without exception. I'll be here all night and when you wake up. I'll accompany you on your morning jog, then on the commute to the Hill. While you're there, I'll remain in your car. Car bombs aren't common, and the Hill garage security is legit, but your campaign manager told me not to take any chances. When you leave the Hill at night, I'll escort you home or wherever else you want to go. Then I'll remain inside your apartment throughout the night again."

I chuckled. "Are you going to sit on the foot of my bed and watch me sleep?"

"Don't be ridiculous. I'll get a chair."

I blinked. "I was joking."

"I'm not. I heard someone tried to kill you this morning."

"That's not supposed to be public knowledge," I said.

"Ms. Hanram wanted me to understand the gravity of the situation. Don't worry. Discretion is my specialty."

It sure is.

"Want me to show you around?" I asked.

Blond hair swung around his eyes as he shook his head. "I already looked up the blueprints. All I need to know is where the coffee machine is."

"It's in the bathroom," I said sarcastically.

He grinned. "I probably deserved that for asking a dumb question, huh?"

We went upstairs. I could feel him just behind me, shadowing me like a good bodyguard. It reminded me of the way he covered me with his body in the hotel. It was only two nights ago. My arms broke out in goosebumps at the memory of his touch...

"If you're watching me throughout the night," I asked, "when do you sleep?"

"I don't sleep much," he admitted. "I'll catch a nap while you're on the Hill."

"Bums sleep in cars," I pointed out.

"Bums and bodyguards! I've had some of my best naps in a reclined car seat."

It felt so strange talking to him in a totally different context. Or, you know, talking to him at *all* rather than having him tease me with what he was about to do to me. But I liked it. Heck, it was nice just to see him with my own eyes without a mask on.

I paused at my bedroom door. "I've had a long day, so I'm going right to bed."

"Can't blame you," he said. He loomed over me, a giant of muscle. "Being attacked can destroy a person's trust in the world. Make them feel vulnerable wherever they go. That's why I'm here." He gripped me by the shoulders to bolster his words. "As long as I'm here, you're safe, Elizabeth."

I loved the way my name sounded on his tongue. We never kissed when we were together. I wondered what his tongue felt like, or those lips...

"Listen," I said, clearing my throat. "I'm not going to be able to sleep with someone sitting in the corner of my bedroom. It's just not going to work. You can hang out in the guest bedroom."

He twisted to look at the door across from my bedroom. "Yeah, alright. I can accept that compromise."

I wasn't sure what else there was to say, so I said, "Goodnight, Ethan."

"Goodnight, Elizabeth."

I went through my evening routine of removing my makeup, applying lotion, and brushing my teeth. I got in bed and stared at the closed bedroom door. My secret lover was right across the hall, and he didn't even know who I was.

I knew I couldn't tell him, but oh did I want to!

Footsteps, then a shadow darkened the light underneath the door. I held my breath. Was Ethan coming inside? Had he somehow figured out who I was, and now was going to take me the way he took me in the hotel room?

I heard the sound of a wooden chair being dragged across the carpet, and then planted outside my door. The wood creaked as he sat in it. Watching right *outside* my door instead of the guest bedroom.

He sure was persistent.

My phone buzzed on the bedside table. A text from Megan.

Megan: You doin okay?

Me: I'm fine. But the bodyguard you hired showed up. He's sitting outside my bedroom door as we speak.

Megan: SHIT. I forgot to call them back and cancel. I'll take care of it.

I texted her back without ever thinking about it.

Me: No! He's fine. I feel safer with him here.

Megan: You sure?

Me: Can't have too many people protecting me, right?

Megan: Glad you're finally taking your safety seriously. I knew you'd come around after a few hours to process everything.

I put my phone away and curled back up with the pillows that still smelled like Anthony. I stared at the shadow underneath my door. I *did* feel safer with Ethan right outside.

What have I gotten myself into?

15

Elizabeth

The next morning my alarm *did* wake me. It was a strange intrusion until I realized what it was, then slapped it to turn it off.

I crawled out of bed. I hadn't even begun my campaign and I was exhausted already. I almost went to open the door, then remembered that I needed to keep him from seeing my tattoos. I quickly put my robe on over my pajamas.

Ethan was sitting in the chair right outside my door. An eReader was in one hand, and a steaming mug of coffee was in the other.

"Morning, sunshine," he said cheerfully.

I took the mug of coffee from him and sighed as the steam hit my face, then took a long sip. It was the perfect drinking temperature.

He arched an eyebrow. "There's a fresh pot in the kitchen."

"Why get myself a cup when you were nice enough to have one waiting?"

He snorted as if that were only half funny. Good lord, his eyes were piercing and vibrant even at this early hour.

"What're you reading?" I asked while sipping more coffee.

"*Sphere*. I'm a big Michael Crichton fan, so I'm going back through all the classics."

It was counterintuitive seeing a massive, muscular bodyguard reading a book. I shook off my assumption. Maybe I needed to avoid judging people by how they looked.

I gulped the rest of the coffee and then went back in my room to change into my running gear. Ethan followed me downstairs and to the front door.

"I'm going for a jog," I told him.

"Yep."

I eyed him up and down. He still wore the same jeans and leather jacket. "Are you going to follow me in that?"

"Why not? I changed into trainers." He lifted

one foot to show off the pair of New Balance sneakers.

"Suit yourself."

Laughter drifted from outside. I opened the door to find Luca waiting for me. Unlike Ethan, he'd switched into proper running attire.

The USCP officer laughed and pointed at him. "Agent Santos was telling me about the time he ate the last bowl of Frosted Flakes in the White House residence."

"Nearly started a nuclear war," Luca said with a tight smile. "POTUS was always grumpy when he didn't have his Frosted Flakes. We never made that mistake again."

"Which one?" Ethan asked. "Which president was that?"

Luca blinked as Ethan stepped into the doorway. "Can't divulge that. Who are you?"

"This is Ethan," I quickly said. "He's my private bodyguard."

Luca stared. "Private bodyguard?"

"My campaign manager insisted."

"Uh huh."

The two of them stared at one another like territorial cats.

"Try to keep up, boys," I said. "I jog like I legislate: fast and without hesitation."

I took off down the steps, forcing them to keep up.

As I ran down the sidewalk of my neighborhood, I forced myself into a stronger pace than normal. I wanted to show these two who was in charge. And to show off a little bit.

Granted, I didn't want to leave them in the dust because I *needed* their protection. Especially on my first jog since the attack. But I wanted them to have to ask me to slow down so they could keep up. It was petty, but I was feeling like a woman who was no longer in control of her life. I needed to be able to *own* something.

Another thing made me run faster: the nagging feeling that, at any moment, the attacker would return and try to finish the job.

Every shadowy alley filled me with a tingling sensation of foreboding. I was absolutely positive a man would jump out of the first alley we came to. I knew it in my bones. The closer we got to the alley, the more certain I became.

And then I passed it, and everything was fine.

Somehow, my two protectors kept up easily. Luca looked like he'd been running his entire life, but Ethan should have been too muscular to maintain this level of cardio. Yet there he was, on my right side, arms pumping as he matched me stride for stride.

He caught me looking, then grinned widely.

"Nice morning for a jog." He was hardly sweating. His cheeks were a little red, but otherwise he had the audacity to look gorgeous while jogging.

Jerk.

"You're not bad, Ethan," Luca said on the other side. "It's actually impressive you can run so fast with that form."

"What the hell is wrong with my form?"

Luca gestured. "You're heel-striking like you're trying to leave craters behind you."

"Oh?" Ethan snorted. "That's better than prancing along like a gazelle."

"You're supposed to land on the balls of your feet," Luca insisted. "That's *proper* running form."

"Proper form is whatever gets you from point A to point B."

"My runs are usually peaceful," I snapped.

That shut them both up.

Nobody jumped out of an alley to mug me this morning, a fact which relieved everyone involved. I made myself a smoothie for breakfast and then showered, did my hair, and put on makeup. That was a full hour-long process. Being a woman sucked sometimes, but if I *didn't* take care of my appearance I'd end up an internet meme, ridiculed until the end of time.

It wasn't fair, but it was the shitty reality.

Ethan seemed unhappy about having to sit in the back seat of my car while Luca drove us to the Hill. And on the other end of things, Luca grinned widely at his displeasure.

"Been a Secret Service agent long?" Ethan asked.

"15 years," Luca replied. He glanced in the rearview mirror. "You been a bodyguard for very long?"

"On and off for a year."

"What other work do you do?" Luca asked.

I perked up to listen to his response.

"I do odd jobs here and there," he said casually. "Handyman stuff around town. Carpentry. Plumbing, especially in the winter."

It took every ounce of willpower in my body not to make a joke about Ethan *cleaning pipes* for money.

"Handyman," Luca mused. "That's quaint. What makes you qualified to be a bodyguard?"

"What makes you so interested all of a sudden?" Ethan asked with a touch of attitude.

"Well, Senator O'Hare has two U.S. Capitol Police officers watching her apartment throughout the day," Luca said. "And I'm a special agent with the Secret Service."

"So?"

"So... Don't you think you're a little

underqualified by comparison?"

"Play nice..." I warned.

"You know, I was thinking about that," Ethan said. "What's a Secret Service agent doing guarding a senator? You running for president or something?"

"Candidates only receive protection once they win a primary," I quickly said. Maybe a little too quickly based on the sideways glance Luca gave me.

"That's what I thought," Ethan said. He leaned forward into the front section of the car, a grin on his face. "You must be a shitty special agent to get downgraded to this kind of work."

"Excuse me?"

"You must've fucked up real bad," Ethan went on. "What happened? You get caught sleeping on the job? Or did you bang the First Lady?"

I waited for Luca to explode at him the way most guys would've, but he only stared straight ahead. "I'm going to pretend I didn't hear that."

"Why? Because it's true?"

"No," Luca responded with icy calm. "Because Secret Service agents are above arguing with 'roided out plumbers."

"The fuck did you say..."

"Stop it!" I snapped.

They both cut off instantly.

"Do you honestly want me reporting to your superiors that you bickered on my detail like a child?" I asked Luca. "Because if you *were* assigned to me as punishment for something, I'm guessing that wouldn't go over very well. And *you*," I said, twisting to face Ethan. "You *do* work for me. One call from a sitting senator and Silver Springs Security will have you out on your ass faster than you can blink. So unless you want to clean old ladies' pipes full time, I suggest you keep your mouth shut."

Both of them were sufficiently cowed. It felt good to let out some justified anger at them. And I *was* a senator. It wouldn't hurt to throw my weight around like that when they were being ridiculous.

"Cleaning old ladies' pipes," Ethan said, chuckling. "That's funny."

I winced. Hopefully he didn't think the pun was intended.

Luca pulled into the underground garage for the Capitol Building. "See you on the other side," Ethan said, giving a mock salute as we left. He crawled into the front seat and reclined the back all the way.

"Asshole," Luca muttered as we walked into the building and through security.

"Give him a break," I said. "He was up all night."

"So were the USCP outside your apartment. Except *they're* qualified to keep you safe. They actually know what they're doing."

I started to dismiss his comment, but then stopped myself. Maybe I was letting my stealth relationship with Ethan cloud my judgement of him as a bodyguard. I hadn't asked about his qualifications. I'd just accepted that he would keep me safe since he was big and muscular.

I accepted him because I wanted him closer to me.

I shook my head. What was I even doing? I should have let Megan dismiss him since I had Luca now. It was reckless letting him stay close to me. He might figure out who I was. But it *did* make me feel safer knowing he was outside my bedroom last night, and I slept so soundly that I barely even heard my alarm.

I need to get control of my life.

That morning, we had an early senate session to debate a budget bill. It was a demonstration of the worst part of politics: it was an endless line of senators attempting to tack riders onto the bill. Pork spending that would help their home states but had nothing to do with the bill itself. Steel subsidies for Pennsylvania; corn research for Iowa.

Politics really pissed me off, sometimes.

Nobody commented on Luca's presence by my side all morning, but I still got plenty of stares. His presence was noted. People were wondering. And when I couldn't see them, I knew they were whispering.

Megan was right that we needed to announce my campaign as soon as possible.

I ducked out of the senate session once my vote was cast. I needed to get an early lunch before the important subcommittee meeting I had at noon. "Hungry?" I asked Luca as we headed to the cafeteria. "My treat."

"Special agents get free meals," he replied.

"Well then it's *really* my treat. Get whatever your heart desires!"

The cafeteria was mostly empty except for a few junior senators and representatives, all glued to their phones while they ate. I sat at a table over by the windows so I could enjoy today's blue sky. It was the first in a while—it had been overcast for practically a month straight. At least snow storms were more mild here than back in Ohio. I did *not* miss lake-effect snow.

My phone buzzed. A text message from Megan.

Megan: Change of plans. We're announcing tomorrow.

Me: What!

Me: Why?

Megan: Some journalists are sniffing around the assassination attempt. Capitol Police can't keep the story under wraps much longer.

Megan: We NEED to time our announcement soon after that news breaks. I'm lining up the events as we speak.

Me: Are you sure it's not too soon?

Megan: Positive. We'll discuss the details tonight. Get your game face on, girl. In 24 hours you'll have more press coverage than Jesus.

She added a GIF of fireworks exploding to the end of the last message.

I stared at my salad. I'd already mentally prepared myself for announcing this weekend. Tomorrow was too soon. I wasn't ready.

Everything was happening too fast.

Luca tried to sit three tables away, but I waved him over. I needed to talk to someone to take my mind off the overwhelming news. "Everyone knows who you are. You might as well sit with me."

He hesitated, then joined me.

"Hey, speaking of being recognized," I said. "Why don't you have one of those ear pieces like the other agents?"

He bit into his club sandwich. "I'm a team of one. There's nobody else to communicate with."

"Oh. I figured they'd be feeding you intel or threats or something at all times."

"Nope."

We shared an uncomfortable silence while he ate his sandwich and I picked at my salad.

"Where are you from?" I asked when the silence became unbearable.

"Kentucky."

I stared at him, unsatisfied with a one-word answer. I'd learned that sometimes a pointed stare could get more information out of a person than a demanding tone.

"Little town called Tollesboro," he grudgingly added. "My father was a hard rock miner."

I grinned. "No kidding! My dad mined coal outside New Alexandria."

Luca's face perked up. "Shitty way to make a living, but it put food on the table for me and my sisters."

"At least you got out," I mentioned. "Most of the boys in my town went straight into the mines as soon as they were old enough to swing a pick."

"Yep," he said.

"That's actually part of the reason I got into politics," I said. "When I was a teenager, I saw a woman speak at our community center. She was trying to get funding for broader adult educational programs in our town. Classes at the library to teach people how to use computers. Help enrolling people in classes at the community college two towns over. Giving people a chance to do more than just toil away at the bottom of a mineshaft."

Luca grunted. "Wish that woman had come to our town."

"Well," I said, "she failed. The funding wasn't approved. *But*, her failure encouraged me to get into politics to help guide money toward programs like that. It was tough with local money when I was on the city council, but once I got into the state senate I had more success. And then by the time I got to Washington I was able to *really* make a difference. Last year we signed a $50 million program to help reeducate coal miners in Ohio, Pennsylvania, West Virginia, and Kentucky."

I couldn't help but brag; it was one of my proudest accomplishments to date. Truly making a difference rather than pointless bureaucracy. Luca looked up at me and I saw admiration in his eyes. Or maybe respect.

"Wish my dad could've done one of those programs," he said.

"He still can!" I said excitedly. "The programs runs through 2025. Or do you mean he's too stubborn to try? That has been our biggest roadblock with many of these programs. Convincing people to actually take advantage of them."

"He died of cancer."

I sucked in my breath. "Oh my God. I'm so

sorry."

Luca shrugged. "Me too. It's been 10 years."

"Lung?" I asked.

His laugh was bitter. "Is there any other kind for a miner?"

I shook my head and ate some more salad. "Now if only we could pass some real healthcare reform."

"If only," he agreed.

Desperate to change the subject from my agent's dead dad, I asked, "You've been an agent for 15 years?"

"Yep."

I stared at him some more until he elaborated.

"I got a full ride to Louisville on a baseball scholarship. Criminal justice. I planned on being a cop, but one of my professors convinced me to apply for the Secret Service on a whim. I never thought I'd get accepted. 15 years later, here I am."

"You like it?" I asked.

He picked at a French fry. "It's what I was made to do," he said with simple certainty. "There's nothing like it. Every day I wake up and keep some of the most important people in our country safe. Every time I walk into the White House I'm awestruck. Even 15 years later."

There was immense pride in his voice. It made

me feel guilty.

"Sorry you have to protect a ditsy senator from Ohio."

"You're not ditsy," he said. "Some people might be fooled by your looks, but you're sharper than most of the politicians I've been around. Plus, you're still one of the most important people in the country."

"So, is it true?" I asked, pushing him now that he was opening up. "You pissed off the wrong person in the White House, and were assigned to me as your punishment?"

He paused before answering. Choosing his words carefully. "A special agent goes where they're told. It's an honor to serve, regardless of the assignment."

"Come on." I leaned forward. "I'm a politician. You can't bullshit me."

He popped the last bit of sandwich in his mouth. "Let's just say I walked in on a powerful person engaged in some... shall we say, *strenuous* political lobbying."

I almost choked on my tea. "Seriously!"

"Yep."

"There's no way you can drop a tease like that without telling me who it was. POTUS?"

His eyes narrowed. "You know I can't tell you."

"The veep? Someone in the cabinet?" I paused, realizing I was making sexist assumptions. "What about

FLOTUS? She *did* just fly back to Arkansas unexpectedly."

"Stop it."

"Okay, okay, okay. You don't have to say it out loud. Just blink or something when I come to the right person. Secretary of the Interior. Secretary of Defense."

"You're relentless!" he said, smiling.

"Secretary of Agriculture. Oh! You blinked! I knew Donaldson was a creep!"

We spent the rest of lunch laughing and teasing one another about which members of the administration were most likely to get caught having sex in the oval office.

16

Elizabeth

I told Luca to meet me over at the subcommittee room while I used the restroom. I almost expected him to insist on following me, but the interior of the Capitol Building was just about as safe as a person could get.

Having lunch with him was a lot of fun. It was nice to get to know the people protecting me. If I ever did become VP, or even POTUS someday, I wanted to make an effort to keep that up. I never wanted to be one of those leaders who ignored all the people around them. I would never let myself become *too good* for that.

I slipped into the restroom by my office to touch up my makeup before the finance subcommittee. I was going to be grilling the banker who was testifying today, and I knew I would be on camera. It was only C-SPAN, but still. I had to look my best.

This bathroom was my favorite because it was close to my office and rarely occupied. It was also quite fancy, with a row of individual makeup mirrors and sitting cushions. Like something Jacqueline Kennedy might have designed.

Touching up makeup gave me some rare moments of peace and quiet. Even if I only got a few minutes of it per day, it was better than nothing.

I was reapplying blush when the restroom door opened. I was annoyed at the intrusion, but didn't glance over to see who it was. I didn't *own* the bathroom, after all. I just hoped nobody else would discover my secret low-traffic restroom.

The person stood just inside the door. They didn't move. Finally I twisted to see who it was.

A man.

In the women's restroom.

Panic washed over me. *An intruder.* And my Secret Service detail was back at the subcommittee...

My alarm turned to relief. "Anthony?"

My favorite U.S. Capitol Policeman gave me a wink, then ducked to check to make sure the stalls were empty. When he confirmed that they were, he fixed me with that same cocky grin.

"Afternoon, Senator O'Hare."

I crossed one leg over the other and gave him a long look up and down his body. "My memory may be fuzzy, but I seem to recall you having the wrong hardware for this bathroom."

"I've got the right hardware for *you*."

"Be that as it may," I said, "why are you here in the women's restroom?"

He strode toward me, starched uniform swishing as he went. He planted his fists on the makeup counter behind me, one on either side of my body, and lowered himself down for a kiss.

God, his lips were warm and sweet and exactly what I needed. I wanted to give in to the feeling, but deep down I knew I shouldn't. Even though he felt so wonderful...

"Anthony," I said, putting a hand on his chest.

"Elizabeth."

"The other night was amazing. The most fun I've had since before I can remember."

"But..." he said. "It sounds like there's a *but* coming."

"*But*, we can't continue this."

"Why not?" he asked teasingly.

"Because I can't afford a political scandal right

now. And neither can you. Right? You said they'd have your head if they found out you weren't at your post when I was attacked."

Anthony's dark eyes sparkled from the lights above the mirror. "It's only a scandal if we get caught. Until then? This is a sexy affair."

He leaned in and kissed my neck, planting his lips down until he reached my collarbone. *Affair.* Good lord, it sounded so hot calling it that. My affair with Anthony.

It would be so easy to give in to him. My body was practically *screaming* at me to surrender to the desire...

"You're not going to want to be around me soon," I said. I wished I could tell him the reason why, because *then* he would truly understand.

"I highly doubt that," he rumbled into my neck.

I shivered as his beard tickled along my skin. "I'm serious. I'm about to be politically radioactive."

He pulled back to look deep in my eyes again. "Then we'd better make the most of it until then."

The voice inside my head disappeared.

He kissed me hard while tugging my skirt up my thighs. His sidearm rubbed against my arm, which was simultaneously alarming and *really* hot. An extra layer of danger to our act.

"Anyone can come in!" I breathed as he pulled

my panties off.

"That's what makes it exciting." He spread my legs on the cushion and looked up at me through his long eyelashes. "You've awoken something in me, senator. I can't help myself."

He buried his face in my sex there in the makeup booth in the restroom. There was no way to stop him; I possessed neither the words nor the willpower. I tried to suppress my moans while his tongue explored my insides but soon I was grunting like a wild animal. By the time he pressed two fingers inside my pussy and focused his mouth on my clit I was clenching my eyes shut, blinded my the pure, forbidden pleasure.

I grabbed a handful of his hair and held him against my sex as I began to come. Just when I thought I wouldn't be able to hold in the cries any longer he clamped his hand over my mouth. Freed from fear, I screamed my ecstasy into his warm palm while he sucked on my clit and rubbed my G-spot with his fingers. My climax was rough and almost painful, wrenched out of my body from the fingers and mouth of a gorgeous, amazing man.

My uniformed lover looked up from between my legs with that same cocky grin. "You're so fucking hot when you come."

I grabbed his head and pulled his lips up to mine, tasting myself on his tongue. "Fuck me," I said. Begged.

"You'd like that, huh?"

"Mmm hmm." I reached for his zipper. I needed to feel him inside me. I wanted to make him come as hard as I had. I needed to see it on his beautiful face.

But Anthony gave me a final kiss on my lips and then backed out of my reach. "That's all for now."

"What?" I gasped.

"I've got to keep you wanting something. Think about *that* until I see you again." He checked himself in the mirror, pausing to straighten his tie. "Take care, Senator O'Hare. I think you're late for your subcommittee."

He left me sitting there in the makeup area, out of breath and spent.

17

Ethan

My superpower was that I could sleep anywhere.

And I mean *anywhere*.

Moving vehicles were a given. Car, train, bus, airplane. You name it. If there was scenery rapidly moving outside the window, I was guaranteed to be asleep within seconds. Didn't matter how much sleep I'd already gotten or if I'd just pounded three cups of espresso. I was *out*.

But I could catch some Zzzs in other places too. A park bench. An office chair. One time I was at a concert at a small indoor venue and I fell asleep leaning against the wall while the opening band played.

Sleeping in a car inside a parking garage? *No problem.*

It worked out well for jobs with strange hours. Staying up all night outside the senator's bedroom was easy when I could grab eight uninterrupted hours in a reclined car seat.

I stretched inside Elizabeth's car and took a sip of the now-cold mug of coffee I'd brought with me this morning. I had no idea when she'd be done on the Hill —her schedule could fluctuate depending on how late the senate session went, or any of her subcommittees. But that was fine, because I had a book to read and time to kill.

I checked my watch, then pulled out my phone and opened the C-SPAN app. They had live video feeds of the senate and house floors, as well as the various subcommittees. I found the Senate Finance feed and launched the video.

Elizabeth's face immediately filled the screen. She was seated behind a curved brown desk with all the other senators on the committee, so I could only see her upper half. There was some color to her cheeks and fire in her eyes.

"*Mr. Thompson, you didn't answer my question,*" she said. The camera cut to the man seated before the committee. The CEO of a bank. "*Your financial institution was given government subsidies to help extend affordable car loans to working class families.*"

"*Senator O'Hare,*" the bank CEO tried interrupting, but Elizabeth wasn't having any of it.

"*These were subsidies you lobbied for. You came before us two years ago and insisted government assistance was the only way you could extend your car loan program. Isn't that right?*"

"Senator O'Hare, what you don't understand—"

"*I understand perfectly well,*" Elizabeth said, venom dripping from every word. "*You begged us for that money, and then turned around and used it to give your top executives larger bonuses. Bonuses which were* —" She paused to review her notes. "*—75% larger than last year, despite a drop in operating income. Isn't that right?*"

Elizabeth tore the CEO apart to the point that he was sweating and fidgety. Part of it was political grandstanding on her part, but it was mostly deserved. I'd read a report four days ago about how that bank was under investigation for bribery and other corrupt business practices.

"Let him have it," I cheered, alone in the car.

When she was done I turned the feed off and leaned back in the seat. I loved being a bodyguard. All in all, it was a reasonably cushy job. It gave me lots of time to read. I didn't stress out too much.

Because that's the thing: most of the job was spent doing nothing. Waiting around for something to go wrong, like a firefighter. Sure, when the senator went for a jog I was suddenly on alert looking for any potential threats, and I kept my ears alert during the night for suspicious sounds. But most of the time, I did jack shit.

My kind of job.

Definitely better than my night job.

It seemed like every dude's dream job. It was mine, when I first found myself being recruited for it. Have sex with women for money. The pay was *outstanding* for a night of work. Honestly, it was usually just an hour or two. Most of our clients were paying for our convenience and discretion. When I was *done* with them, they wanted me gone.

$5,000 a pop for that? Hell fucking *yes*.

But it had its drawbacks. Meaningless sex with women with deep checkbooks wasn't very fulfilling. Most of them took their pleasure however they desired it and then sent me home. I liked that just fine at first, but after a while it got old. It sounded corny, but sometimes a guy wanted to cuddle.

Over time, it became a grind. Just like any 9-to-5 job. *Punch-in*, do your work, then *punch-out*.

Until *she* came along.

My client from the other night had ruined me. Being with her wasn't like being with other women. We had *chemistry*. Something special beyond just two people exchanging money for services rendered.

The first time she booked me, I'd thrown her on the bed, dragged her ass to the edge, and then fucked her for all I was worth. That's how the file said she wanted it: hard and fast and without any pleasantries.

But she was *hot*. An hourglass figure and tits so beautiful they looked carved from marble. The mask accentuated the pleasure, like we were doing something dangerous. More dangerous than someone hiring a male hooker. Her pussy had gripped my cock so tight that I almost came before she did. *That* would have been embarrassing for an escort in my business. And when I did come, it was like she sapped every ounce of moisture from my body.

This woman left me fucking *dehydrated*.

I couldn't wait until she booked me again. Her schedule, so far, was once a week. I still had four or five days to go.

Unless she's done with me.

The fear was persistent in the back of my head. There were a lot of guys to choose from in this business. Guys who were every bit as jacked or handsome as I was. More so. She had her pick of all of them.

What if she eventually got bored of me, and wanted to try something different?

Elizabeth and the Secret Service prick came out of the elevator up ahead. I pushed my thoughts about the mystery client aside. Daydreaming like that was a good way to get sloppy, and eventually fired.

Focus on Elizabeth. Think about the client later.

Luca opened the driver door. I gave him a sickly-sweet smile. "Anyone get shot on your watch, *agent?*"

"You catch anyone out here while snoozing?" He sniffed the air. "It smells like a homeless person in here."

"Easy," Elizabeth warned as she got in the back seat. "If I have to listen to the two of you bicker on the ride home I'll shoot *myself* in the head."

The dark humor made me laugh so hard that Luca turned and waited for me to stop before driving out of the parking garage.

There were two new USCP officers outside Elizabeth's house tonight; one in the car and the other seated by the front door.

"See you tomorrow, *special agent*," I said as Luca stopped short of the steps. "One suggestion? A different tie. Dark colors don't go well with your complexion."

I turned and went inside before he could say anything else.

Elizabeth sighed at me. "I was joking about shooting myself in the head, but the more I listen to you two, the more appealing it sounds."

"Sorry," I said. "I've had guys like that looking down on me my whole life. I've learned to bite back."

"Guys like him?" she asked.

"You know the type," I said. "That dude was definitely prom king at his high school back in 1950, or whenever he graduated. Probably got a sports scholarship to a D1 school. And not in football. In a preppy sport, like lacrosse."

The smile Elizabeth was trying to suppress told me I was right.

I took a shower and changed clothes while it was still barely light out. As stereotypical as it sounded, night was the biggest danger to someone like Elizabeth. During the day an intruder would have a tough time getting by the eyes of the two officers outside. At night, it would be much easier.

"Megan's grabbing Mexican on the way in," Elizabeth called when I came downstairs. "What do you want?"

"Whatever you're having," I said.

She put her hands on her hips, showing off her figure. She was a *very* good looking woman. "You don't want to think for yourself?"

"I'm easy."

"If you say so," she said, as if I would regret it later.

Her campaign manager, Megan Hanram, came over half an hour later. When I answered the door she dropped her bag of Mexican food and leaned back to get a long look at me. The kind that construction workers gave women who walked by a build site.

"Hello," I said. She was young and attractive herself, and it never got old having a woman look at me this way. I worked hard to keep my body looking this way.

"Hello to *you*," she said. "I wish I was an intruder so you could handcuff me. Do you have handcuffs? I can get some handcuffs if you don't."

Elizabeth groaned from the kitchen. "Stop harassing my bodyguard!"

Megan winked at me and slipped through the doorway, ensuring that she rubbed against half my body in the process. I shared a smile with the female officer on the porch and closed the door.

In the other room Megan said, "I can see why you changed your mind about keeping him."

"Megan!"

"Just saying. He's not hard on the eyes."

I grabbed my food from the kitchen—which ended up being three spicy enchiladas, refried beans, and rice—and carried it back to the hall to eat. Elizabeth had told me that they were going to discuss some things I wasn't privy too. I didn't mind. Hell, I was used to confidentiality in my job—as a bodyguard *and* as an escort.

I took a bite from one of the enchiladas and glanced toward the kitchen. Elizabeth was watching me with a funny look on her face. The kind Megan had given me. I stared back coolly. Did she have the hots for me? Why was she still staring? This was getting weird...

Then the spiciness from the enchiladas kicked in.

"Oh," I said with surprise. Elizabeth smiled. "Oh! Oh no!"

"Yep," she called from the other room.

"What the actual fuck? My mouth is on fire!"

"Ghost peppers will do that," she said, carrying a bottle of beer over to my chair. "I don't have milk, but this might help."

I guzzled it down. It didn't help at all.

I managed to pull apart my enchiladas and pick out the tiny ghost pepper pieces. The food was edible after that, though my mouth remained damaged for the rest of the meal.

Eventually the senator and her campaign manager stopped giggling at my pain and got to work. They both crowded around their laptops, speaking softly while going over stacks of documents.

The sun set, and the night crawled onward.

I had a new respect for politicians. Elizabeth had gotten up early for her jog and breakfast, then got to the Hill before most of her colleagues. After working there all day she got home and continued working with her campaign manager. I was exhausted just *watching* her work.

I could never have a job like that. I would lose my mind.

I finished dinner and went into the kitchen to make a pot of coffee. Both of them stopped chatting while I was there, like whatever they were discussing was top secret. What subcommittees was Elizabeth on? I knew the intelligence and foreign affairs committees handled sensitive information, but the finance committee was supposed to be boring.

Then again, it was Al Capone's tax returns which brought him down. There was something to be said for following the money.

I drank a cup of coffee and finished reading *Sphere* while they worked, then got started on *The Andromeda Strain*. There was something warm and comforting about reading a book you'd already read years ago. Like hugging an old friend after a long separation. Yeah, you knew how it would feel, but it felt good nonetheless.

It was 10:00 when Megan gathered her things and left. "Make sure you guard her *body*," she said to me as she headed for the front door.

"I hear that joke on every single job I work," I said.

That wiped the smile off her face. "Well, fuck. And here I thought I was witty. G'night, Elizabeth!"

The door opened and closed, and then it was quiet.

Elizabeth gathered her things from the kitchen table, putting the laptop and papers back into her bag. Somehow, she didn't even look tired. She was a machine.

I couldn't help but admire her. There was something incredibly sexy about a woman who was at the top of her profession. Hard-working and dedicated. And *gorgeous.* When I first saw her, I assumed she got elected solely based on her looks. Obviously I'd been wrong.

She was really good at what she did. I didn't need to sit in on a session in the senate to know *that.*

Yet as sexy as she was, I kept those sorts of thoughts at bay. She was the client. I was here to protect her, not admire her. This wasn't my escort job.

But man, if she was one of my clients...

"Ethan," she called suddenly. "Come have a drink with me."

I picked up my beer bottle. "Still working on this one."

She bent over to retrieve something from a lower cabinet, showing off that perfectly round ass pressed tight inside her pencil skirt. She came up with a bottle of something brown, which she waved at me enticingly.

"Something stronger than beer."

I grimaced. "Alcohol makes it awfully tough to stay awake all night."

"Irish coffee it is, then!" She gave me a look. "Come on. I need a stiff drink after four hours with Megan, and I don't want to drink alone."

I took a deep breath. One drink wouldn't kill me. Especially if there was caffeine with it.

I joined her in the kitchen and watched her stir cream liqueur into a mug with coffee, then add a healthy pour of the liquor—which ended up being Jameson Whiskey. She poured two fingers into a cup for herself, neat, then raised her glass to me. "Cheers."

"Bottom's up," I said, clinking my glass to hers.

She sighed as if she'd been looking forward to the drink all day. After the last 24 hours of excitement, she probably had been.

"I'm sorry Agent Santos is getting under your skin," she said. "I can see why it would turn into a pissing contest between you two."

"And I'm sorry he's an uptight asshole," I said, adding a smile to take away the sting of the words.

Elizabeth squinted at me. "You're not helping, you know."

"Hey, I really need this bodyguard gig to go over well. I'm doing my best to make it stick. And it's a lot harder with someone like *him* punching down at me the whole time."

She studied her drink. "You don't like your other job?" She met my eyes. "The handyman stuff, I mean. You said it was carpentry? And some plumbing?"

I'd almost forgotten the fake story I'd given her. I shrugged. "It's alright."

"Just alright?"

I almost wanted to tell her the truth about what I did. That I was hired by rich women to meet in expensive hotels and perform elaborate, toe-curling sex acts on them. But she was a senator, and she'd almost certainly fire me immediately. A prostitute as a bodyguard would be political suicide. She'd have no choice.

"It's just..." I said, looking for the words to help her understand without giving anything away. "I don't know. It's just not very fulfilling. I'm just going through the motions every day, waiting for it to end. It's meaningless."

"Meaningless," she repeated.

I took another sip of coffee. The liquor had bite to it. "I want more than that. I want to do something that leaves me satisfied at the end of the day! Protecting a senator? That's the kind of work I could look forward to every morning. Fulfilling." I gestured at her with my glass. "You're one of the most powerful women in Washington. Protecting you is a reason to get out of bed every morning. Much more fulfilling than my *other* job."

My comment was meant to flatter her, but she seemed disappointed. Almost hurt.

"I see," she said.

What did I say?

She knocked back the rest of her drink even

though she'd just poured it. Mine was still almost completely full.

"I'm going to bed," she said in a small voice. "Goodnight."

She walked away.

"Did I say something wrong?" I asked, following her into the living room.

"No. I'm just suddenly very tired."

There was more here. I was missing something. What nerve had I struck? She reached the stairs and began climbing. I wanted to follow her, to apologize for whatever I had said, but I didn't want to push my luck.

So I let her go and cursed myself for being an idiot, even if I didn't know why.

I turned to go back into the kitchen... And that's when I saw it. On the mantle above the fireplace.

It had a charcoal-colored fabric base, with gold embroidery around the outside. The eyes were wide and cat-like. It shone there on the mantle, reflecting the light just right. Practically glistening.

A Venetian mask. One I was intimately familiar with.

How had I not seen it before?

I went to the mantle and picked it up with trembling hands. It might have been any other mask bought at a costume shop, except cloth had been sewn into it to cover the eye holes. I rubbed my thumb over the design, feeling the curves where it had covered her cheeks and face.

This was it. I knew it with a certainty that bordered on the supernatural.

I turned, and she was there in front of me. Elizabeth. Senator O'Hare.

My mystery client.

18

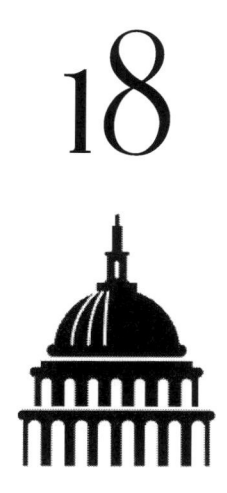

Elizabeth

The blood in my veins ran cold. Ethan was holding the mask. His eyes were wide with realization.

He's discovered who I am.

I was such a fool. The man I was keeping around as my bodyguard, the man who I'd been paying for sex in a hotel room, had finally discovered who I was.

Because *of course* he had. He was bound to eventually. Whether from my tattoos, or the smell of my perfume, or any other clue. The mask was just the most obvious, stupid thing for me to leave out.

"I can explain," I began.

He snatched my arm and pulled up my sleeve, revealing the tattoos on my right arm. His touch sent electricity up my body.

"It's you."

I took a step back and held out my hands. "My campaign manager booked you as a bodyguard, not me. It was a total coincidence. I should have fired you the moment I recognized you on the porch, before you found out, but I thought…"

He was staring at me intently. What was going on behind those piercing emerald eyes?

"You thought what?" he asked.

My throat was tightening, making it difficult to speak. "I'm sorry your escort job is so terrible," I whispered. "I shouldn't have allowed myself to think… To believe that you might…"

I couldn't say the words. They were too painful now that he'd told me the truth. That he *hated* his job as an escort. That it was a job he took no pleasure in.

"Elizabeth," he said, letting the mask drop to the floor. "I've dreamed of you."

"Don't say that," I said. "Don't lie to make me feel better."

There were tears in my eyes. Why did this hurt so much? He was an escort. Of course he didn't care about me. I was just a paycheck to him.

But then he made the pain go away.

"Elizabeth." He took my hand in his and looked deep into my eyes. "I *don't* enjoy my other job. It wears me down every time. Except for one part. One client who makes it all worth it. Who I've been dreaming of every night since she first hired me five weeks ago."

I held my breath.

"You, Elizabeth," he said. "There is only you."

His lips touched mine and electricity passed through us. A thousand electrocutions tingling my nerves and making me weak. But he drew me up into his arms, carrying me forward and then lowering me to the ground until the soft carpet pressed against my back and his hot, hard, wide body blocked out all the light.

"Ethan..." I moaned.

He removed my skirt, gently rather than with the forceful exuberance of our clandestine hotel pairings. He was caring as he slipped my panties over my knees and ankles, and then removed his own pants. His cock slid inside me like it had half a dozen times before, yet completely different.

In the hotel room we'd *fucked*. Here we were making love.

"Elizabeth."

My name on his tongue was a curse and a prayer, a whisper and a scream. It held all the emotion that had built up between us over the last month.

Exploding into his lips and fingertips and the rock hard sensation of his cock inside me.

I wrapped my legs around him tight, desperate to feel every inch of him.

"Elizabeth," he said again. "I've wanted you so much."

"Yes."

"I've yearned to stare into your eyes..."

"Yes!"

"To kiss you on the lips..."

"Yes!"

"To make love to you slowly and passionately, like we have all the time in the world."

"*Yes*," I moaned, drinking in the sight of him on top of me. "Yes, Ethan, *yes*, I've wanted all of that too."

Somehow he felt larger inside me than normal. Swollen with lust so that he filled every inch of me from the inside, filled me to the brim, there was no room for more.

And then the most incredible thing happened. My lover's eyes widened and he moved faster. His hand cupped my cheek and then grabbed onto my hair, and his hard jaw worked in silent screams. Ethan's orgasm was almost painful with its urgency as he pushed himself as deep as he could go inside me, giving all of himself to me while he cried out in my apartment.

I moaned and gripped his face tightly, viewing every second of his ecstasy with voyeuristic enthusiasm. Here was the evidence I'd wanted so badly. In the hotel room, Ethan could last for hours. When he was fucking a client he could hold himself back.

When he was making love to me, here with our eyes and lips and hands locked together? Here, he was only a man, and I was only a woman.

His woman.

*

"You knew this whole time?" he asked.

We were laying on the floor of my living room, a throw blanket covering half our bodies. I was distantly aware that at any moment one of the USCP officers could come inside, or even Luca, but I couldn't bring myself to care.

I traced a finger over the lines of his muscles. "I mean, I *did* pick you out of a digital catalog. I knew it was you the moment you showed up on my porch."

"And you didn't say anything."

"How could I! There's a reason I wore that mask to our meetings. I happen to work over at that big building downtown. You know, the one with the rotunda and 534 other politicians inside? Across from the big pointy obelisk thingy?"

He shoved me playfully. "I guess I'm just shocked you kept me around. A smart politician would have sent me away immediately."

I sighed. "Yeah, I should've."

"Why didn't you?"

I felt myself blush, then got pissed off at my body for reacting that way. "I don't know."

"I have an idea." He rolled over, putting his face an inch away from mine. "You like me."

"Maybe a little."

He began to sing in his deep voice. "Ethan and the senator, sitting in a tree. K-I-S-S-I-N-G..."

"Shut up!"

We laughed and wrapped our arms around each other and kissed on the floor. I wanted to touch every inch of him. Examine all his nooks and crannies. It felt like luxury after being forced to wear a mask every time.

"So, you don't like your escort job?"

He shrugged. "I mean, it's alright. It could be worse."

"But you love being with me."

"Oh yeah. Big time."

"I bet you say that to all your clients."

"Yeah," he replied, rolling his emerald eyes. "Sex with you is all fine and good, but what I *really* prefer is being with all the older, wrinkled women married to millionaires who don't know how to please them sexually. That's what really gets me off."

"Yeah, yeah," I said. "You've made your point."

His fingers ran through my hair and his face drew serious. "I've been afraid you would get bored of me."

"Really?"

"We'd been together five times, and you have an entire catalog of escorts to choose from. All of them are practically supermodels. Every time I leave the hotel room, I'm terrified it will be the last time I get to see you."

I made my face into a mask of puzzlement. "You know, that's a good point. I forgot about all the other hot guys I could be paying to fuck me. Let me go grab my laptop and find one of *them* to be my bodyguard."

I started to rise but he wrapped his arms around me and pulled me back to the ground.

"I wouldn't do that," I said softly. "You and I have... I don't know. A special kind of chemistry."

A grin split his beautiful face. "I couldn't agree more."

"Now that we're on the subject," I said. "Who are some of your other clients?"

"Elizabeth..."

"Is it anyone I know? I know a lot of women in

this town." I paused. "I know a lot of men, too. Are you ever hired by men? Do escorts do that?"

He narrowed his eyes at me. "Some do. I only service women."

"Then tell me who some of them are. Give me the juicy details!"

"You know discretion is the most important part of this business," he said calmly. "How can you trust that I'll keep your secret if I'm blabbing about other clients?"

"Because your other clients aren't *special*, like me," I teased. "Just tell me one! That's all. Who were you with last week?"

"Nobody. Just you, on Saturday."

"What about the week before that?"

"Still just you."

I frowned. "Is business that bad? Or is the escort industry seasonal? Nobody wants to go out in the snow to get fucked by chiseled hot men?"

But he didn't laugh at the joke. His face was serious as he regarded me.

"Elizabeth, I haven't been with anyone else. Not since you first hired me."

I almost laughed. "What?"

"You... I don't know. You broke me. Before, I could fake enthusiasm for all of my clients just fine.

Now?" He pushed up onto an elbow and caressed my cheek. "How can I fake chemistry with other clients after feeling the real thing with you? I'm not that good of an actor."

"Ethan..."

He smiled. "For the last five weeks, there has only been you, Elizabeth."

We kissed, this time soft and sweet. Lovers who were meeting again after a few days apart. A kiss of reuniting.

"Your boss lets you do that?" I asked.

He laughed and laid back down with his hands behind his head. "Yes and no. I told the company I didn't want to be hired by anyone but you. It pissed them off. They sent me emails twice a day insisting I open my schedule up to more clients again. In fact, when they sent me to your hotel the other night I was afraid it might be someone else."

"You did seem extra excited that night," I admitted.

"You have that effect on me."

Laying there with my cheek against his chest, I felt safer than I ever had in my life. Nothing else in the world existed. Just two lovers pressed together with a carpet digging into their asses.

But the real world had a way of ruining the most perfect moments.

I sighed. "The timing of this isn't great."

"Why?"

Because I'm about to run for president. I almost blurted it out. Ethan made me feel like I could be honest around him. I felt like I could trust him.

"We're going back to Ohio tomorrow," I said.

"When were you going to tell your dashing bodyguard?"

"I'm telling you now."

"What's in Ohio?"

"Some constituent meetings," I lied. "I'm also giving a speech about an upcoming bill. Oh, and depending on when the story breaks, we'll probably end up giving a statement about my assassination attempt."

I glanced up at Ethan. He was staring off, the gears in his head turning faster and faster. Then his eyes widened.

"You're running for president!"

I almost had a heart attack. "What?"

He pushed up into a sitting position, forcing me off his chest. "The hushed meetings with your campaign manager. The grandstanding you did in the finance committee yesterday."

"You were watching that?"

"And now this sudden, unannounced trip to Ohio. Candidates always go back home to announce."

He bobbed his head up and down. "You're totally about to announce your candidacy."

Shit. Shit shit shit. He'd figured it out. Should I keep lying and insist he was wrong? There wasn't much of a point since he would find out tomorrow regardless. And I *did* feel like I could trust him.

But more than that, I had all this emotion boiling inside my chest. Excitement and anxiety and fear. I *needed* to tell someone. I had to get it out.

"I'm running for *vice* president," I clarified. "That's my goal: make a splash with my campaign, then get picked as a running-mate for another candidate."

"Why not try to get the nomination yourself?" he asked.

"You're sweet," I muttered. "I just turned 35. I don't have enough experience. Running on someone else's ticket would do a better job springboarding me into a real chance of winning in eight years."

He folded his arms around his legs and stared at the wall. "Picking you as a running mate would give them Ohio. Plus you're young, attractive..."

"Hey! I'm more than that!"

He patted my bare thigh. "You didn't let me finish! You're also charismatic, hard-working, and *very* good at what you do. Watching you dismantle that banking CEO today was a treat. When I was hired to be your bodyguard, I spent a few hours making phone calls to people around the Hill. Getting information on you before I came by your apartment. You know what most people said?"

"That I have a nice pair of tits?" I joked, sticking my chest out to give him an eyeful.

"Every single person I spoke with said you were incredibly competent. One of the smartest senators on the Hill. And that you're not a woman anyone should underestimate."

I grinned. It felt good hearing this kind of feedback from someone other than my campaign manager. Sometimes a girl liked to be complimented. I was only human.

"I think your campaign will do very well," he said.

"I hope so," I replied. "Since we're announcing tomorrow, this is probably the last normal night I'll ever have."

He frowned. "So, I'm not judging you. But having kinky sex with male escorts in hotel rooms is the kind of thing that sinks a political campaign."

"No kidding," I muttered.

"Does your campaign manager know?"

"Hell no. She'd literally kill me." I poked him in the chest. "So you'd better not tell her. Or anyone else, for that matter."

He grinned a mischievous grin. "Make me."

19

Elizabeth

Make me, Ethan had said with a mischievous grin. Waiting to see what I would do.

I smiled back sweetly.

I rolled him over and grabbed his cock with tight fingers. I loomed over him like a lioness about to make the killing bite to its prey. He looked up at me as I kissed his chest, pecking each individual abdominal muscle like I was playing *connect-the-dots*. I paused just over his cock, which was already rock-hard again from my touch alone, and stared up at his gorgeous face.

His mouth was agape and he breathed heavily, waiting for what I would do.

I flicked my tongue out like a snake. Brushing just the tippy-tip of his head with a scant few taste buds from my tongue. His entire body shuddered, a low earthquake through his muscular legs that vibrated my body. I flicked out again, and again, touching a little more of his sensitive skin with each one.

"What do you want?" I asked innocently. I wanted to hear him say it. *Beg* for it.

"Baby, you know what I want."

"I really don't," I said. "I'm just a dumb politician. You have to spell it out for me."

He gritted his teeth. "I want *you*."

"You want me to what?"

"I want you to suck my dick," he breathed.

I wrapped my lips as tight as I could around his head. *Just* the head. I looked up at him and hummed, "Hmm?"

"I want you to suck my dick with those gorgeous lips."

I went down another inch.

"I've dreamed about your pretty little lips," he said in a throaty voice. "What they looked like behind that mask."

Another inch.

"Those lips are better than anything I could have imagined. The way they fit so tight around my hard shaft, all the way down, oh my *God*..."

He trailed off in a long moan as I deep-throated all the way down to his base—until my lower lips pressed against the beginning of his balls. His head rubbed against the back of my throat, but I was blessed with both a high political acumen *and* a lack of a gag reflex. Every bit of him was inside my mouth.

Every. Single. Inch.

"Holy fuck!" he cried out in surprise and lust. "Oh my God!"

I pulled all the way off and then gave his head a little kiss. "Tell me you'll keep my secret."

"Baby, I'll do whatever you want. If you asked me to rob a bank right now I wouldn't ask any questions."

"That's what I like to hear."

I went back down on him, deep throating him in long, caressing strokes. I wanted to make him come again as quickly as possible. More proof that I wasn't just another client to him. With each tight-lipped stroke it became more of a challenge for me. Usually sex with a man was about trying to *keep* him from coming too quickly.

It was a delicious change of pace to try to urge him to his climax as fast as possible.

I ran my fingernails over his chest with one hand and cupped his balls with the other. Caressing them gently. Then at the bottom of one stroke, with

Ethan's cock all the way down my throat, I stuck my tongue out and licked his balls. The sound he made was feral.

The faster I went, the more noise he made. He practically squirmed underneath my sensual touch. Soon he was grabbing a handful of hair and forcing my head down on him. Holding me there while my lips were tight around his base.

"I'm gonna come in that pretty mouth," he breathed. "Are you gonna be a good little whore and take every drop?"

"Mmm hmm," I moaned into his thick meat.

"Oh. Oh! *Ohhhhhh...*"

He spasmed and held my head down as hard as he could with both hands, pinning my lips against the skin around his base. The hot spurt of his seed was like a shower of praise, proof of his true attraction for me. Validation of my sexuality as a woman.

He held me there long after he came. Then the muscles in his arms and body released their tension, and he relaxed back on the ground. Slowly I pulled myself off his rod, ending with a soft kiss on the tip.

"I love how strong you are," I said. "I love that you're not afraid to be a little rough."

His grin was relaxed. "I love the way you have no gag reflex."

"I thought you would."

He picked up the mask off the floor and examined it. "I hated this thing. I wanted to see your face so badly. You have no idea how much I've wanted to see those lips wrapped tight around me."

I crawled up his body and kissed him. "These lips?"

"Those are the ones."

I ran my thumb over the bones of his cheek. Along his hard jawline. Savoring how beautiful he looked on the floor of my living room.

"I'm hungry for a snack," I said. "You want something?"

I tried to get up, but he snatched my arm and held me down. "I'm not done with you yet," he said in a dark voice.

"You're not?" I said doubtfully. I rubbed my knee against his still hard cock. "Three times in such quick succession..."

His smile showed teeth. Like an animal that had finally found its prey. "You have that effect over me."

He flipped me over onto my hands and knees, then positioned himself behind me. One quick thrust and he filled me again, as deep into my lower lips as he'd been in my mouth.

"I don't want a snack," he said. "I want *this*."

He grabbed hold of my shoulders and fucked me hard, each thrust sending shockwaves through my body. He was still as hard as stone despite coming twice in the last 15 minutes, and that fact alone drove me more wild than his passionate assertiveness.

He fucked me fiercely on the carpet. The kind of sex where our skin slapped together and we were both sweating from the effort. The kind where it was difficult to tell where my moans ended and his began.

"I'm close," he said as our cries reached a frenzied intensity. "But I don't want to come yet."

He slowed down and then wrapped his arms around me, pulling me backward against his chest. He rested back on his haunches, keeping me pressed tight against him. Then he kissed my neck and began pumping his hips up into me.

"Ohhh, right there," I said as this new angle hit my G-spot. "Don't stop."

"Wouldn't dream of it," he purred in my ear.

With every thrust he tightened his arms around me. One around my chest and the other around my neck, the bicep squeezing against my neck the way it had in the hotel room during our last encounter. The louder I cried the tighter he squeezed until he was practically choking me with his muscles, a python constricting me with his passion.

When his other hand slipped down between my legs and pressed hard against my special button? I saw colors no human had ever *seen* before.

My final screams were so loud I was shocked the

Capitol Policewoman didn't burst into the apartment to check on me.

Thank goodness she didn't.

20

Elizabeth

Ethan insisted on remaining professional—he sent me to bed and stood watch outside my bedroom door. Which was probably for the best, considering how things had turned out with Anthony. As much as I would have enjoyed Ethan sharing my bed for *actual* sleep, leaving his post was too risky.

Which was just fine, because I slept like I was dead. Or, more accurately, like a woman who'd had her brains fucked out.

I skipped my run the next morning. There was too much to do preparing for the trip to Ohio. Bags to pack, speeches to go over. Megan came over at 5:00am and we spent a full hour arguing about what outfit to wear for the announcement itself. Shoes and jewelry choices were another half hour.

Sometimes I envied men their simplicity. Choosing what color tie to wear was about as complicated as men's fashion got.

Ethan played it cool throughout the morning. He sipped his coffee while watching the front door. I even heard him making friendly conversation with the USCP officers on the porch. And whenever I walked by to grab something from the kitchen or out of my coat closet, he only smiled at me.

But that smile held far more than just friendliness.

Luca was waiting on the porch when we left, looking sharp in his suit and tie. Ethan gave him a mocking salute as we went down to the waiting cars.

We landed in Columbus later that morning. Megan was a flurry of phone calls the moment we touched down. She was also a flurry of cursing in between calls.

"Fucking fuckheads," she muttered while we walked down the airport terminal. "That was the Washington Post asking me for a comment on their story. It's going to drop at any moment."

I glanced at my watch. "Two hours until the event. That's the perfect amount of time to build up buzz in the media before we announce."

"What story is breaking?" Luca asked, keeping stride with me while looking around for threats. "The assassination attempt?"

"Yep."

"Why does the timing of your speech matter?"

Ethan let out a bitter laugh. "He hasn't figured it out?"

"Don't be a dick," I hissed. Ethan only winked.

"What haven't I figured out?" Luca demanded. He stopped looking for threats and stared at us intently. "It's crucial to your protection that I'm given all available information."

I shared a look with Megan, who nodded slightly. Although Luca was a nice guy, he *was* sent to me by POTUS. If we told him about my campaign announcement, he might report that back up the chain. That would give POTUS an opportunity to upstage me. Make a sudden announcement in the rose garden.

Granted, if POTUS suspected I was going to announce my candidacy he could do all that anyways, but we didn't want to make it that much more obvious.

"It's unrelated to Senator O'Hare," Megan told Luca. "You have the details of our public event today. The crowd size and the venue and the Columbus Police plans. Focus on that, please."

Luca's face was blank as he resumed searching for threats.

Two cars waited for us outside the terminal. Megan and Luca shared one car with me while Ethan was delegated to the other car with one of Megan's assistants.

Our first stop was as frustrating as it was necessary: the hair salon. I needed a trim and wanted to add some color to my hair prior to the announcement. Or rather, Megan insisted I needed those. Appearance was important for a politician. The photos taken today would be some of the most important of my life. I had to look my best.

Luca remained outside the front door of the salon the entire time. Ethan took a seat across from me and flipped through a Cosmo magazine while sending me the occasional sexy smile.

Then we were back in the cars and heading to the event itself at the Ohio Statehouse. I stared out the window at the scenery as a motorcycle passed our cars on the left. It felt good to be back home, but in a different sort of way. This wasn't a homecoming. It was a beginning.

The beginning of the rest of my life.

A Google alert buzzed on my phone. The news was out.

ASSASSINATION ATTEMPT ON OHIO SENATOR

I showed the article to Megan. "I like the photo they used. They got my good side."

Megan snorted. "You're welcome. You should have seen the photo they originally chose before I called in a favor at the Post to get it switched."

My phone started going crazy with emails and text messages. Some were from friends. Some were from family, even though I'd called my parents to tell them what had happened already. It was like a constant vibration in my lap, too many notifications to read.

And it was only going to get worse once I announced. My life would never be the same again.

My phone made a different sort of vibration. A phone call from a Northern Virginia area code.

"Should I answer any calls from reporters?" I asked.

"Yes!" Megan immediately said. "But don't give anything away. Just tell them to watch your public statement at 1:00. The more build-up for that, the better. Go on! Answer it."

I put the phone to my ear. "Senator O'Hare speaking."

"*Hey there, sugar,*" came a deep, familiar voice.

Anthony!

I glanced at Megan and then lowered my voice. "How did you get my number?"

"*That's not hard for Capitol Police.*" There was

a strange static noise in the background. Like a hairdryer blowing. "*Just calling to say I miss you.*"

My stomach tingled. I missed him too, even though I just saw him yesterday in the Hill restroom. And even though I'd been with Ethan last night. "I miss you too," I whispered. "Is that the only reason you called? I'm kind of busy right now."

"*I also called to say you look good.*"

"I know you think I look good," I said.

"*No,*" he insisted. "*I mean you look good right now. I like what they did to your hair.*"

I froze, then looked around. It took several seconds to realize the motorcycle that had passed us before was right in front of us.

"Are you here? In Ohio?" I demanded.

"*Hopped on my bike the second I saw the event pop up on your events page,*" Anthony said. I could hear the smile in his voice. "*It was a pleasant six hour ride from D.C. Little cold, though.*"

I fought down the rising excitement at having him here. The Capitol Policeman who had a crush on me had followed me all the way to Ohio. At the drop of a hat. Like a sexy shadow.

"Anthony!" I hissed. "I don't have time for this."

The motorcycle up ahead slowed down, dropping back until our car caught up to it. He evened out his speed when he was right next to my window. It was a Japanese bike, not his police cruiser, and he wore padded motorcycle armor from head to toe. He turned his helmet to face me, though all I could see was the tinted glass.

"*I'll leave you alone,*" he said. "*Just wanted to let you know I was here. Yeah, you've got that bodyguard and the Secret Service detail covering your ass, but a third set of eyes can't hurt. I'll be in the crowd during your speech looking for threats. Knock 'em dead, sugar.*"

"Thank you," I said, and meant it.

Anthony's motorcycle suddenly shot forward, racing up the highway.

Megan glanced at me. "Was that a reporter?"

I gave a start. "I don't know who it was. Just a biker I guess, looking over at who was in our car..."

Megan stared at me like I was speaking Greek. "On the phone. Was that a reporter on the phone?"

"Oh." I shook my head. "Just my cousin. He saw I was making a speech and wants to be there, but it's too far of a drive up from New Alexandria."

"That's nice," Megan said dismissively before returning to her own phone call. "Goddamnit, Parker. Just send your best reporter to the event. Trust me, the Columbus Dispatch is going to want someone there. Have I ever steered you wrong?"

I watched Anthony's motorcycle shrink in the

distance as we neared downtown Columbus.

"Uh oh," Luca said from the front seat.

"What is it?"

He held out his phone for me to see. "We have a major problem."

21

Anthony

I couldn't get her out of my head.

She was like an addiction. Or the aftertaste of a bite of chocolate cake lingering on your tongue, reminding me that I wanted more. Constantly occupying my attention.

I was never the kind of guy to get too attached to women. Usually I went on a couple of dates, the woman tried to get closer to me, and then I broke things off. I liked it that way. Physical more than emotional. Things were *simpler* that way.

But nothing about Elizabeth was simple.

She was different. She wasn't like any of the other women I'd been with. I *wanted* to be emotional with her. It's like she'd opened the door to part of my soul which had never been touched, and now she was walking around dusting off all the furniture. Making herself at home.

I *craved* Elizabeth. Being apart from her was so painful that I'd spent the last two nights watching her apartment from down the block, even though two other USCP officers were assigned to her protection. That's why I accosted her in the restroom at the Capitol Building, just to taste her sweet sex even for a few minutes. It's why I then lingered outside the Finance Committee door and listened to her grill that banker, just to hear her voice.

It was why I'd gotten up at 6:00 in the morning to drive straight to Ohio on my bike.

There was no thought involved. I was running on a combination of impulse and desire.

I would find a way to get her alone again. And when I did, I would fuck the stress out of her until she was cool and relaxed.

Until then, I would help protect her at the public speech at the Ohio Statehouse. Because I may not love Elizabeth yet, but I knew, deep down, that I was *falling* in love with her.

And people in love did crazy, stupid things.

I raced ahead on my motorcycle to get there ahead of everyone else.

22

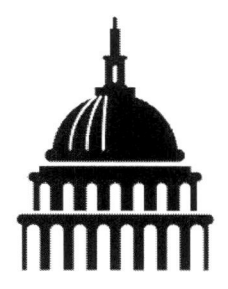

Elizabeth

"What problem?" I asked.

Luca waved his phone. "The problem is Columbus PD are only sending nine officers to the event."

Megan's mouth hung open. "So fucking what?"

"I requested 14 from them," Luca replied. "Minimum."

"Nine sounds like plenty," Megan said, returning her attention to her phone.

"For an event this size? Absolutely not," Luca insisted. "Three to four officers operating the metal detectors at the entrance. Six more for general perimeter duty. Three at each entrance to the stage. Not to mention patrols inside the crowd itself, or on the roofs of surrounding buildings..."

"You're overreacting," I said.

"We need to postpone the event." Luca twisted back around and began to make a phone call. "I'm going to speak with the Chief of Police and demand they put spotters on the roofs of the nearby buildings."

"Absolutely not!" Megan suddenly snapped. She grabbed Luca's shoulder tightly. "There is no way we are postponing the event. We'll lose a huge chunk of media coverage."

"You can't sacrifice security for press time!" Luca said.

"No," Megan replied. "What we can't sacrifice is political opportunity just because you're paranoid. Columbus PD is in charge of security for the event. You're in charge of protecting Senator O'Hare's person. Focus on that, agent."

Luca looked like he wanted to argue more, but turned back around and stared out the window.

The Ohio Statehouse was in downtown Columbus, two blocks from the Scioto River. The facade was beautiful Greek architecture, stone columns supporting a long, wide roof. A statue of William McKinley, the 25th President, stood high above the lawn.

"Should we mention McKinley in the speech?" I asked. "I didn't even think about him."

Megan shook her head. "Absolutely not. He was not a popular president. Also, he was *successfully* assassinated in office. Not quite the connection we want people making."

"Good point."

The streets on three sides of the Statehouse were blocked off with barricades and a large crowd of people was being funneled through the metal detectors into the fenced-off lawn area. There were so many people. At least a thousand. More than could fit into the lawn.

That was a great sign. This event was going to get lots of attention.

A podium stood at the top of the steps, positioned between two of the massive stone columns. Balloons and streamers were everywhere in varying shades of red, white, and blue. Curtains were erected on either side of the building, like a makeshift theater stage where crew and aides could wait without being seen by the crowd. And above the building was a long banner, currently covered with a sheet.

"What do you think?" Megan handed me her phone. It showed a picture of the banner at the print shop. 2020 O'HARE, except the last zero and the O in my name blended together in offsetting colors.

"I love it," I said, feeling a lump form in my throat. "It's like I always dreamed."

"This isn't a dream," Megan said. "This is the real deal. Get your game face on."

We were allowed through security and then parked on the side of the Statehouse, then walked up to the stage behind the curtain. I peeked around the edge at the milling crowd, which had already filled the entire lawn and was crammed along the side streets outside the perimeter. There were *thousands* of people here.

"Called in a few favors to let the crowd fill the streets," Megan said with pride. "An overflowing crowd will look great in the photos." She looked at her watch. "I'm heading down to the press box to watch. I want to be available for questions immediately after your speech. There's going to be a lot of excitement!"

I was going to be alone. I'd given hundreds of speeches before, but this one was on another level. The most important speech of my life.

"It's going to be weird not having you behind me," I said. "Watching from behind the curtain, fist-pumping every time the crowd cheers."

"You don't need me. You've got these two strapping men to keep you company." She winked at Ethan, who grinned back at her. "Don't forget that the confetti will shoot off once the speech is over. It'll be loud. Don't let it spook you. If you flinch, it will make you look jumpy and weak. The point of this public announcement is to show you're *not* scared."

"You mean *pretend* I'm not scared?" I said with a nervous laugh. "Because I'm definitely a little scared."

Her smile softened. "Me too, Elizabeth."

We held each in a long hug. We'd come a long way together. And yet we were just getting started. When we pulled away, Megan had to wipe a tear from her eye.

"Remember, project strength," she said. "Stand right behind the podium, waving and smiling, until the mayor comes back out to join you. Then you'll leave together. You've got this!"

She walked away, leaving me feeling very alone.

"Senator O'Hare," Luca said with surprising formality, "I need to reiterate that I am unhappy with the level of security for this event. I am just one agent. I cannot guarantee your protection at an event this open."

I gave him a smile. "You look good wearing sunglasses. Like a real Secret Service Agent."

"Ma'am," he said. "I'm serious."

"We're past canceling the event. This is happening."

"It's a bad idea," he warned.

"I appreciate your honesty. Now if you'll excuse me, I need to mentally prepare for my speech."

I turned away. Luca sighed, then approached Ethan.

"Listen. I know we don't get along, but we need to put that aside for her safety. Her speech is set to run about five minutes. If you hear any sort of gunshot, it's crucial to first protect her with your body, keep her low, and then escort her out of the open. If I am incapacitated, it's crucial to get the senator around the corner to the side street where the car is waiting. Don't let yourself get blocked off."

I expected Ethan to say something sarcastic. He surprised me by nodding. "I'll do my best."

I smiled. They were putting aside their petty annoyances for my protection. It gave me a warm tingling in my stomach, and made me feel less alone.

Luca slipped behind the curtain to go around to the other side of the stage. I leaned out toward the podium, where the Columbus mayor was currently giving his speech to the crowd, warming them up before I went out. Going over my long history of public service for the great state of Ohio.

"Nervous?" Ethan asked over my shoulder. He stood almost as close to me as someone possibly could without actually touching. I could feel his warm breath on the back of my neck.

I snorted. "Why would I be nervous? It's only the most important speech of my career. One misspoken word or awkward eye-twitch and everything goes down the drain. No reason to be nervous at all."

Ethan poked me with something. "This'll help."

It was a metal flask, wrapped with fine leather. The initials E-J-J were stamped into the leather.

"If this is supposed to be a gift, you got my

initials wrong," I said.

"The flask is mine. The contents are for you. A little liquid courage before the most important speech of your career."

I unscrewed the cap and took a long pull without thinking. Fire ran down my throat, scouring everything it touched. But it warmed my belly, and it did make me feel a little more confident.

"I never made fun of you for using your real name," I whispered. "In the hotels."

He shrugged. "It made it feel more real to me. Though I never had that problem with you. It was always real with you, Elizabeth."

It would have been easy to kiss him then and there. But of course that would be disastrous. A senator making out with her bodyguard before announcing her presidency.

But I *did* want to kiss him. I decided there would be much more time for that later, consequences be damned.

"Now I just need to figure out your middle name," I said. "I bet it's Jacob. Ethan Jacob Jacobs. That silly name fits you."

His handsome face smirked. "Guess again."

"Ethan *Jessica* Jacobs?"

He arched an eyebrow. "I don't think I'm pretty enough for that."

"Don't sell yourself so short."

He hesitated like he wanted to hug me, then gave me a reassuring pat on the shoulder. "You were made for this. It'll be easy. Just be yourself. You hear that crowd? They love you."

He was right: the crowd was roaring right now. It was a weekday, and freezing outside, and yet thousands of people had come out here to see *me*. Their senator.

Hopefully I can become their vice president, and beyond.

The mayor reached the end of his speech, announcing my name. The crowd noise rose to a deafening level.

I put on my best smile and strode toward the podium.

23

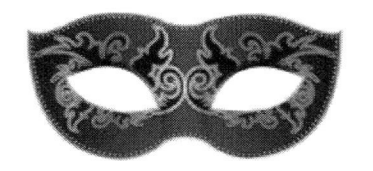

Ethan

Elizabeth was incredible. She was so many things all at once: a savvy politician, a caring senator, an intelligent orator, a beautiful woman.

While watching her walk onto the stage, I came to a realization that would forever change my life.

I'm in love with her.

It was stupid. Ridiculous. I'd stared into her eyes for scarcely more than a day. Spoken to her for two days.

I'd been with her longer, though. I felt like I'd known her for years. And even though I had so much more to learn about her, I couldn't wait to start.

I took up my position at the edge of the

curtain, opposite of Luca on the other side. I pulled my eyes off the gorgeous senator and began scanning the crowd for anything unusual.

"That's the Ohio welcome I'm used to!" Elizabeth said into the microphone, voice enhanced by the speakers all around. The sound echoed off the far buildings. "It always feels great coming home to the state I love."

Power was sexy. It was as true for women as it was for men. There were so many things I loved about Elizabeth, but I was quickly discovering that her power enhanced all of it. It made her beauty that much more beautiful, her intelligence even more sharp. Like a spotlight shone on an already breathtaking statue.

What was going to happen to us? In about five minutes she would officially be running for president. She couldn't keep fucking her bodyguard on the campaign trail. It was too risky.

Granted, she *was* single. Maybe we could make things more official. I could be her boyfriend. Would having someone like that help or hurt her political chances?

Does she want that?

I still had this nagging fear that she only liked me physically. Just a man she paid to fuck her in a hotel room, and leave immediately after. Which brought up the most important point of all: my history as an escort would torpedo her chances. If we started dating publicly, it would come out. There was no way it could remain a secret under the magnifying glass of scrutiny that came from a presidential campaign. And that would sink her chances.

While watching her give her speech before a roaring, adoring crowd, I came to a sad realization. I couldn't be with her. Even if she wanted to be with me too, it was too risky. I couldn't allow it to go on. It would threaten all of her dreams.

I have to break things off for good.

The realization made me sad, but I knew it was the only option. Even if it meant quitting this job and bringing in a different bodyguard. That way there wouldn't even be the temptation for either of us.

My scanning eyes locked onto someone in the crowd. Wearing all black. Was that...?

Icy fingers gripped my heart and squeezed tight.

Yes. I was certain it was them. And if they were here, Elizabeth was likely in danger.

I tried to get Luca's attention, but he was busy scanning the crowd. I had to take care of this myself.

I slipped back behind the curtain and around the side. Down the steps leading away from the building, then around into the crowd by the front.

"By now, many of you have heard the news," Elizabeth was saying.

Nobody in the crowd noticed me jostling past them. They were mesmerized by Elizabeth's speech. She truly had a gift for oration. She held the crowd's attention like she was announcing lottery numbers.

One person up ahead wasn't paying attention. A shady-looking guy who was moving through the crowd, not paying any attention to the senator behind the podium.

"Yes, it's true," Elizabeth said. "Earlier this week, I was attacked."

The crowd gasped.

"But it's going to take a lot more than some harassment on my morning jog to stop *this* senator from representing the great state of Ohio!"

The crowd roared. People raised signs and bounced up and down, blocking my view of the man I was pursuing.

There. He'd turned right, and was moving toward the stage now.

Toward Elizabeth.

"And that is why I am here today, in front of all of you, on the steps of the Ohio Statehouse."

It was tough pushing through the crowd, but I was gaining on him. Now that I was close I knew it was him. Recognized the clothes from earlier. The crowd parted for a split second, and I saw that he was holding something down at his side.

Something black and metallic.

"Today, before all of my constituents..."

I shoved people out of the way to reach the attacker. He was dangerously close to the stage now. Within shooting distance.

He stopped, then raised the black object.

"...announce my candidacy for President of the United States!"

I launched myself, tackling him from behind.

People around us shouted with surprise, but they were drowned out by the roar of the crowd at Elizabeth's announcement.

The man fell forward and I landed on top of him with all my weight. The object from his hand went flying, hitting someone in the back and clattering to the ground. A walkie-talkie.

I stared at the shiny plastic object while the crowd roared around us. *Not a gun*. Was I mistaken? I eased my weight off the guy and rolled him over. He was wearing the same motorcycle armor as the guy who had buzzed by our motorcade, and then hovered around Elizabeth's car for far too long. He had dark hair that was shaved on the sides of his head and thicker on top, with a thin black beard along his jaw. Tattoos ran down the side of his neck into his motorcycle gear.

The *pop* of confetti cannons went off, filling the air with tiny bits of colored paper. Balloons rose into the air, and the enormous 2020'HARE banner was unfurled above the Statehouse. Elizabeth beamed out at the adoring crowd.

I grabbed the guy by his motorcycle jacket. "Who the hell are you, and why are you stalking the senator?"

"Get off me!"

He tried to fight me but there was no chance with my full weight pinning him down. "Answer me!"

He gritted his teeth. "My breast pocket."

"What?"

"Open it, fuckhead!"

I hesitated only a moment before unbuttoning the outer pocket. A rectangle of leather was inside, smooth on one side and adorned with metal on the other. The gold badge of a United States Capitol Police officer.

What the fuck?

"I was on her detail earlier this week," the officer growled. "I'm here watching Elizabeth. Trying to keep her safe!"

He wasn't trying to kill her. He was here for the same reason I was. Relief washed over me.

And then the gunshots went off.

24

Luca

I had worked with some very powerful people in my career, but I really admired Senator Elizabeth O'Hare.

She was strong and confident for someone so young. Incredibly intelligent. She was self-aware, too, which was rare for a politician. She knew her strengths and limitations.

She had a bright future ahead of her. I found myself hoping that someday she would run for president.

I glanced over at Ethan.

I gave a start. Where had he gone? I spotted him a few seconds later, jostling through the crowd.

Goddamnit, what are you doing?

He was pursuing something. Or someone. Taking a moment to put aside my annoyance, I scanned the crowd ahead of him. *There.* A man was pushing sideways through the crowd. He wore all black, and he was now making his way closer to the stage.

The urge to sound the alarm was strong, to grab Elizabeth and guide her off stage to where it was safe. I fought down the urge. There were always a dozen potential threats at events like this who ended up being harmless. It was probably just a guy trying to get a better view.

Ethan was gaining on him. The stranger stopped, then raised a walkie-talkie to his mouth. Was he a plain-clothes Columbus PD officer?

Ethan flew through the air, tackling the suspect. Maybe he saw something I didn't. Nobody else noticed because at that moment Elizabeth reached the climax of her speech.

"...candidacy for President of the United States!"

I blinked.

You have got to be kidding me. That was what all the whispering and secrecy was about. Why they cared more about the speech than security. She was announcing her candidacy today!

"Goddamnit," I muttered to myself. That was something I would have liked to know prior to setting up her security.

Confetti cannons went off, and Elizabeth didn't flinch at all. Balloons rose into the air like a rising tide of latex colors. Above, strings snapped and a giant banner unfurled. The crowd roared even louder.

And then a single gunshot cut through the noise.

It was a sound I knew immediately. One we were trained to know. It echoed off the buildings around the square, a whip-crack like thunder.

I began running toward Elizabeth.

A second gunshot rang out, then a third. Two balloons rising into the air in front of Elizabeth burst, and I heard a bullet ricochet off the stone wall behind her.

The crowd realized what the sound was, and then everything turned to chaos.

"GET DOWN!" I screamed.

Elizabeth still stood proud behind the podium, forcing herself not to flinch at what she probably thought were the confetti cannons. The three seconds it took me to reach her felt like three hours. I don't know how she wasn't cut down then and there, but I wrapped my arms around her and put my body between hers and the crowd.

Another gunshot. I tensed, waiting for the impact that would send me to my grave. None came.

"This way," I said, covering her and pushing her toward the curtains at the edge of the stage.

"What?" she asked, dazed. "What was *that?*"

We reached the concealment of the curtain, and I pulled myself off her body. Now that we were no longer out in the open I could take stock of the situation. Our escape route was guarded by two policewomen, so the best thing for us to—

Two more gunshots pierced the curtain a yard from Elizabeth, leaving two eye-holes in the fabric. Like a child's Halloween costume.

"We need to get out of here, ma'am!"

The chaos intensified as I put an arm around her and guided her toward the side street where our cars were waiting. Two Columbus police flanked the mayor ahead of us.

"Luca," Elizabeth said. She looked at me with a pale face.

"Just relax and we'll get you to safety, ma'am," I said.

"Luca. I've been shot."

25

Elizabeth

I didn't remember being shot.

One minute I was standing behind the podium, doing my best not to flinch at the endless confetti cannons going off, and the next minute Luca was smothering me with his body and leading me away. When we got behind the curtain, I realized my hip and thigh were wet. When I touched my side my palm came back a shade of red so deep it was almost black.

"She's hit!" Luca roared. "The senator has been hit!"

Our escape to the side street was abruptly halted. Luca lowered me to the ground behind a column and ripped the fabric of my skirt, my favorite skirt, the one I'd insisted on wearing for the important day. But Luca didn't seem to care about the skirt because he was shouting for help, and there was so much blood now staining my clothes, and it was funny because I didn't even feel it.

Then the world went black.

Everything was a blur.

Shouting. Yelling.

The inside of an ambulance.

Lights that were so bright they hurt my eyes.

Faces crowding my vision, asking me questions.

The tearing sound of bandages being cut.

Then everything went black again, and when I opened my eyes I was somewhere else, with even more police around me.

I started to panic, and called out for help, but then someone poked me in the leg with a needle and everything became fuzzy and warm.

I blinked, and then I was inside of a car.

The back seat of a car, staring up at the black fabric and the plastic light.

I tried to take a deep breath but was unable. I wiggled my arms but they were tied down. In fact, I could move nothing. I was tied down.

Restrained.

I've been kidnapped.

"What..." I said.

"You're awake!" the driver said.

"Let me out," I demanded, thrashing harder. "Let me the hell out of here! I'm a United States Senator!"

"Hold on. It's me, Agent Santos. Just relax. I'm pulling over."

I heard gravel crunching as we slowed down and stopped on the side of the road. Cars whizzed by outside, and I suppressed the urge to call for help.

It was difficult to think. *Agent Santos.* That was Luca. The Secret Service Agent assigned to me. He was my protector.

The door opened and he unclipped my restraints. No, not restraints. Seat belts.

"Only way to keep you from rolling onto the wound while asleep," he said. "Sorry if it scared you."

I rose to a sitting position, which made me dizzy. "No. It's okay. I wasn't scared," I said, even though I was trembling.

Luca squinted down into my eyes. "How do you feel?"

"Tired," I said immediately. "My eyes feel crusted together. How long..."

"We've been driving for two hours," he said.

I looked at the sun behind him. It was falling in the sky. It was late afternoon.

Had I been out all afternoon?

"Let's get back on the road and I'll catch you up to speed," he said.

I got out so I could move to the front seat. That's when I noticed that I was wearing baggy hospital scrubs over my lower half, though I still wore my expensive blouse and jewelry on top. Before sitting down, I twisted and looked at my side. There was no blood, and only a single bandage the size of a credit card above my hip. And there was no pain.

I sat down and closed the door. "I was shot," I said out loud.

"Yeah..." Luca looked over his shoulder before driving the car back onto the highway. "Just a glancing shot, thank God. Probably a ricochet. Took a thumb-sized chunk out of your love-handle, but nothing worse."

"I... I don't have love-handles," I said. I suddenly felt self-conscious in my hospital scrubs.

"Just a figure of speech. We got you medical attention at Grant Hospital, but then I received orders to take you to an undisclosed location."

"Undisclosed location?"

"For your protection. Elizabeth? Someone tried to kill you today. A sniper. You're lucky to be alive."

I tried to grab onto the thought but it slipped away. Someone else had tried to attack me. Okay.

"Where are we going?"

"You'll see when we get there."

I tried reaching into my pocket before realizing I didn't have any. "Where's my phone?"

Luca grimaced. "I'm afraid we had to leave that in Columbus. There's a high probability you're being tracked that way. I've got your suitcase in the trunk, though. You can change when we get to where we're going."

"Where are the others?" I asked. "Ethan?"

"Ethan's not coming with us."

"What? Why not? Is he..." My throat tightened at the thought of anything happening to him...

"Ethan tackled a suspect in the crowd," Luca answered. He almost sounded proud of the bodyguard. "Might've been a spotter for the real shooter, who was using a high caliber rifle from a window in the PWC building. I take back everything I said about that meathead."

"Spotter." My head still felt like it was full of cotton. It was tough to focus on any one thought. "Why would they need a spotter?"

"Lots of reasons. Determining if you're wearing a bulletproof vest. Looking for other targets, like the mayor. The spotter might have been a backup option in case the sniper missed. Could have jumped up on stage to finish you off. In any case, this suspect was seen following our cars from the beauty salon to the event. That's too much of a coincidence for them to be innocent."

A memory tugged at me from the car ride, but my head was too fuzzy and it slipped away like mist.

"Someone tried to kill you," Luca said, deathly serious. "Once you're in the secure location we'll discuss our strategy going forward. But first, we're picking someone up along the way."

"Who?"

"Someone who will help me keep you safe."

26

Elizabeth

"It's a puppy!" I squealed.

The black Labrador Retriever came galloping down the driveway toward me, tongue hanging out. I crouched down and he licked my face, then circled around me while getting as many sniffs in as he could. The whole time his entire butt wiggled back and forth along with his tail.

He reached the wound at my side, then paused to sniff at it. After that he licked my face extra careful.

We were at a little farmhouse in the middle of nowhere. The moment Luca unlocked the front door the dog came running out. He didn't even say hi to

Luca—he came straight to me.

"Nice to see you too," Luca muttered, crouching down to scratch the dog's ear.

"Whose dog is this?"

"Boomer is mine," he said. "My sister watches him most of the year while I'm in Washington."

"Boomer," I said. He flopped onto his back to show me his belly, which I gave some vigorous rubbing. "Are you named that because you shoot off like a cannon the moment anyone opens the door?"

Luca scratched his head. "My, uh, wife named him. She went to Oklahoma. Boomer Sooner."

"Oh," I said. "I didn't realize you were married."

"Divorced. Hey, Boomer? Want to go for a ride in the car?"

The dog leaped up and went right in the passenger door, then climbed across to the back seat where he promptly sat on his haunches like he was waiting for the bus.

"Boomer'll keep you safer than three of me," Luca said. "Let's get back on the road."

"I'm not going to meet your sister?"

He shook his weary head. "I told her not to be here when I came by. Said it was a national emergency. She knows not to ask questions about my job."

My first reaction was mild relief. In my ultra-baggy hospital scrubs and bloodied blouse, I wasn't in a condition to meet anyone.

My second reaction was: *national emergency?*

I supposed it was the right phrase for it. I'd had two separate assassination attempts in a 72 hour period. Surprisingly, that realization didn't make me curl into the fetal position on the ground. I was too busy to deal with this bullshit. I had a campaign to launch. I didn't have time for assassins.

Yeah, it was callous with maybe a hint of denial, but if Megan were here she would have said the exact same thing.

"Nobody else is here?" I asked.

"Nope."

I popped the trunk on the car. "Then turn around so I can change into some proper clothes."

It wasn't as good as a shower, but getting into some fresh clothes did wonders for my morale. I actually felt like *myself* once I was wearing slacks and a long-sleeve button-up.

"We're not going to an office building," Luca said when he saw what I was wearing.

"This is the most casual thing I have aside from pajamas," I said. "Where *are* we going?"

"You'll see."

We got back in the car and drove south for another hour. I didn't realize how *boring* a car ride could be without a cell phone to keep you occupied. It was especially frustrating since I was itching to read news about my campaign announcement and how the networks were reacting. Was I trending on Twitter? And if so, was it because of the candidacy announcement or the assassination attempt?

But it gave me time to silently process everything. I was still coming down from the painkillers so it was good to sort through everything in my head.

We reached Wheelersburg, which was on the border with Kentucky, then headed east from there. We wound down unmarked, unpaved roads for almost half an hour before reaching a tiny little cabin in the middle of nowhere.

"Whose place is this?"

"Mine." Luca turned the car off and got out. "Well, my family's. Use it for hunting in the winter. Not so much since my dad died. Haven't gotten around to selling it. But the primary benefit is there's nobody around for 20 miles in any direction."

The cabin was on a little hill, giving me a view of the surrounding terrain. It was nothing but endless trees and rolling hills everywhere I looked.

The cabin itself was a single-room building. A living room, sleeping area, and kitchen occupied the 40-by-40 foot space, plus what looked like a bathroom off the back of the kitchen. That was a relief; I had begun to fear this place didn't have plumbing. I'd rather get killed by assassins than do my business in an outhouse.

Boomer trotted inside, jumped onto the sofa, and rested his blocky head on his paws.

"It's freezing in here!" I said, wrapping my arms around myself. "I swear it's actually colder inside than outside."

"I'll get the generator running, then the heater," Luca said. He went to turn off the faucets in the kitchen and bathroom, which had been left at a drip to prevent freezing.

"I don't suppose there's hot water for a shower," I grumbled.

"Actually, we have a tankless water heater. You can have a hot shower as soon as I get the generator up."

"Agent Santos," I said with fake seriousness. "If I don't take a scalding hot shower in the next 60 seconds I'm going to literally die. Then you'll have to report to your superiors that a senator died on your watch."

He grinned. "Wouldn't want that, would we, ma'am?"

The generator was a loud rumble on the back side of the cabin, but if it meant I could take a shower I didn't care. The bathroom was small but featured an oversized claw-footed tub long enough to stretch out in. I considered soaking in a hot bath but decided a shower was more practical. The moment the steam and water hit my body I sighed with pleasure. I had to turn sideways to keep the water from hitting my bandage, but that was fine because mostly I was just standing under the water to let the heat thaw out my bones. Once I felt like a human again I toweled off and changed into my pajamas.

The sun had set by the time I went back out into the main room. Everything glowed with orange light from old light bulbs, giving the cabin a cozy feel. The ceiling was steepled, with thick wooden rafters running across the air above. In other circumstances this might have been a pleasant vacation stay.

"This casual enough for you?" I said, spreading my arms and twirling like a model.

"Much better." Luca opened one or two cabinets and nodded approvingly. "We've still got some dry goods from the last time I was out here. I can hunt and fish for some other fresh meat. Should hold us out for a week."

"A week!"

"Or two," he said. "My orders were vague."

"I thought I would only be here for... I don't know..." I threw my hands in the air. "A day at most!"

He came out of the kitchen. "How about we sit down and discuss that."

"I don't want to sit down," I said. "I want to get back to civilization so I can *do my job.*"

"You can't do your job if you're dead," he said through gritted teeth.

"I'd rather be dead than useless. Luca, I can't just hide away with my tail between my legs. I just announced my candidacy for president!"

"Something you neglected to tell me." Anger suddenly filled his handsome face, and frustration shone in those experienced eyes. "I needed to know as much information as possible in order to keep you safe. And you kept the most important detail from me!"

"It was supposed to be a secret..." I began.

"A secret?" His laugh was bitter. "Do you seriously think I would run around telling everyone that you were about to announce your candidacy? Do you not understand what a Secret Service Agent does?"

At the time, it had made sense since we were afraid he might tell his superiors. But now it seemed ridiculous for us to have kept it from him.

He paced back and forth in his suit. "I was operating without knowing the full picture. And you almost died. They nearly killed you, Elizabeth!"

He shrugged out of his dress jacket, revealing his white dress shirt underneath. I gasped at what I saw. "Luca. Are you..."

He looked down at himself. "It's not *my* blood, Elizabeth."

All annoyance I felt instantly disappeared. Here I was worrying about a few days of delay when I had very nearly died earlier today. *Luca* had very nearly died: he'd shielded my body with his without hesitation. Protecting me. He was literally covered in my blood because he possibly saved my life.

"I'm sorry," I said in a small voice. "I should have told you."

He gave a jerky nod, but refused to meet my gaze. He was incredibly handsome in that moment, still wearing his dress clothes but covered in the evidence of his desire to protect me.

The events of the day were still a blur, but bits and pieces began coming back to me. How Luca had immediately put himself between me and the shooter. The way he pulled my head down against his stomach while he scrambled over to the curtain, keeping my head as safe as possible. Pressing his hands on my wound while staring into my eyes and screaming at the top of his lungs for assistance.

Carrying me in his arms toward safety.

"Luca," I said. "You saved my life today."

"I did my job today," he snapped. "In spite of the roadblocks."

"I might be dead if not for you. You shielded me, then got me to safety."

He put his hands on his hips. The dress shirt was tight against his muscular chest and arms, muscles I hadn't noticed before, and sandy hair fell across his light eyes. "I did what any agent would have done to protect their assignment."

"But it wasn't *any agent*," I said, taking a step

toward him. "It was you. Agent Luca Santos."

All the tension left his face. Like my acknowledgment was what he'd needed to hear. "I thought you were dead."

"I wasn't."

"There was so much blood," he said, staring at the ground. There was a tremble in his voice now. Not fear, but something close. "I thought for sure it was a gut wound before I got a better look at it."

I stopped when I was standing in front of him. "Were you afraid of failing your mission?"

"Yes," he said. "But it was more than that." He finally met my gaze fully. His eyes were sharp. Certain. "After seeing your speech in front of that crowd, I... I see something in you now, Elizabeth. You're not just some normal politician. You know what scared me more than failing my mission? I was afraid that the world was losing something special."

Me. He meant me. I was something special.

So I kissed him.

His lips were salty and warm, his skin weathered with experience. He resisted for the tiniest fraction of time, but then he gave in and kissed me back, grabbing the back of my head tightly and holding me close against his lips like he would die if I pulled away...

Boomer lifted his head and growled.

"Easy," I said, turning. "No need to get jealous,

buddy."

Luca whipped his head toward the door. "It's not you. He hears something." He drew his sidearm. "Someone's outside the cabin."

27

Luca

Whatever I felt during our kiss—incredible, transformative, tantalizing feelings—disappeared as soon as Boomer growled.

My sidearm was in my hand before I realized it. "Stay here. Keep away from the windows."

I didn't wait for her to comply. I opened the front door a crack. Frigid air rushed inside. I paused, straining my ears. All I heard was the rustling of the trees in the wind.

"Lock the door behind us," I said, then slipped outside with Boomer.

He paused to sniff the air, then stalked off into the trees. I followed at a steady pace, ducking low and moving from trunk to trunk for cover. Clouds covered the moon, making the woods a deep black. Whoever was out there might be the same professional who had shot at Elizabeth at the Ohio Statehouse. If so, did they have night vision goggles? Were they watching me carefully while I stumbled through the underbrush from tree to tree?

I ignored my fear as I followed Boomer. The land sloped down away from the cabin. My feet slipped on leaves with every step, threatening to send me crashing to the ground. But I had to keep up with my dog. I'd gladly trade my own life for Elizabeth's, but if anything happened to Boomer...

He stopped ahead, crouching low with his tail stiff. He blended in almost perfectly in the darkness, like a wolf. A low growl rumbled from his throat.

Whatever had caused the noise was up ahead.

I raised my gun and looked down the barrel. My orders were clear: bring the senator out here and shoot anyone who approached. No questions asked. None of our neighbors would have stumbled onto our land by mistake. Not this far from the property line.

If I saw a person, they were getting a cluster of three bullets straight to the chest.

I steadied my breath as I moved forward, Boomer at my side. Without my coat I was terribly cold, but years of training kept my hands steady on the gun.

There, up ahead. A bit of white cloth sticking out from behind a tree. A person hiding. I aimed my pistol.

"You have one chance to come out before I shoot."

I wasn't being truthful. I intended to shoot them the moment they stood, regardless of who they were. I just wanted to make it easier on myself. Get a clear shot.

The person twitched. Leaves rustled, and Boomer's growl deepened.

The person shot out from behind the tree, running away from us. But it was immediately obvious from the motion that it wasn't a person. An animal. Boomer shot after it at full speed, disappearing into the darkness. I jogged after him and found the white cloth stuck on a shrub: it was the white wrapper from a fast food burger. In the distance I heard Boomer barking, and the hiss-chitter of a raccoon.

I sighed and called Boomer back.

It took the entire walk back to the cabin for my heartbeat to return to normal. Boomer panted and wagged his tail like he was a good boy. "You *are* a good boy," I said, scratching his head as we walked. "But next time save it for a bad guy, alright?"

Boomer's open-mouthed smile told me he intended to do no such thing.

I knocked on the door and Elizabeth answered

soon after. "You should have verified it was me before opening up," I said.

"I saw you approach from the window."

"And I told you to stay away from the windows," I said with more annoyance than I meant.

Elizabeth paused. "Sorry. I was worried."

"It's okay this time. But you need to listen to what I say."

"Okay."

She was looking at me intently, which is when I remembered what had happened before I went outside. *The kiss.* A moment of weakness.

"I'll get started on dinner," I said. She started following me, so I added, "You can use my cell phone as a Wi-Fi hotspot to check the news. Assuming I have a cell signal."

"Oh!"

She was like a kid on Christmas morning who'd finally been told she could unwrap her presents. She ran to her suitcase, fished out her laptop, and sat down at the kitchen table. I told her the hotspot password for my phone and she was a flurry of typing and mouse-clicks.

"I'm still trending on social media!" she exclaimed excitedly. "Both #OHARE2020 and #assassination hashtags are still in the Top 10. I bet Megan is losing her mind with excitement."

"Wow," I said while gathering ingredients. Canned chicken and some boiled rice. I didn't have much in the way of sauces here, but I did have salt, pepper, and butter. That would have to do.

While Elizabeth made excited noises, I couldn't stop thinking about the kiss. It was a mistake, obviously. She was my assignment. I was supposed to keep her safe! Any other feelings would only get in the way of my job.

But I want her badly.

I took deep breaths and tried to think logically. This was a normal reaction between two people who shared a traumatic event. It would fade once we got some sleep. I had to acknowledge it, and move past it.

As if it's that simple.

She chatted about her campaign while we ate our simple dinner, the kiss long forgotten. The types of policies they were going to emphasize, and which other primary candidates they hoped to hitch their wagon to. The preliminary polling data on Elizabeth's popularity, both in Ohio and in the other 49 states.

Yet as I made up the couch and wished her goodnight, I couldn't get her out of my head.

I woke up early the next morning to make coffee and get dressed. When I came out of the bathroom, the senator was standing there with her hands on her hips.

"Where are you going?"

"Hunting," I said. "We're out of canned chicken."

She frowned, which somehow made her look *more* beautiful. "It's okay for you to leave me here while you're out in the woods?"

"Well, I'm scouting the perimeter too," I replied. "Checking for game trails or other signs of recent activity. Boomer can keep you safe."

She crossed her arms under her breasts. They were full against the soft fabric of her pajamas. The look she gave me was the kind which made bankers and political opponents wither.

"There's no way I'm staying here alone," she said in a calm voice. "I'm going with you."

I could tell arguing with her would get me nowhere. Plus, it *would* be safer for her if she tagged along.

I found some of my sister's clothes in the storage chest that fit Elizabeth pretty well. Jeans, a flannel shirt, and a heavy double-lined jacket. A beanie hat completed the wardrobe, causing her honey-colored hair to spill down around her shoulders.

"No neon hunting vest?" she asked.

I pulled down one of the hunting rifles from the rack on the wall. "Not today. Anyone we come across out there is *not* someone we want seeing us."

"What about a gun for me?"

I raised an eyebrow. "You ever hunted before?"

"No, but there are people trying to kill me. I'd feel much safer with my own weapon. I promise not to shoot you."

Again, there was no point in arguing so I pulled down the second rifle and gave her a quick lesson on all the important parts.

We trudged through the woods as the sun rose over the treetops. Our air clouded in front of us with each breath. As Boomer ran out ahead of us he left a trail of puffed respiration in his wake, like a black lab steam train.

"What are we hunting?"

"Deer," I said. "Plenty out this time of year. Best part of owning a few hundred acres that we rarely use is the deer feel safer here. They flee other hunting areas and congregate on our land. Shouldn't have any trouble finding some."

We walked in peaceful silence for 20 minutes before reaching the deer blind. It was a simple wooden structure 30 feet up in a tree, like a dilapidated tree house. I slung my rifle over my shoulder and climbed the ladder, with Elizabeth right behind me.

"Cozy," she said while ducking inside. The ceiling was too low for a person to stand, and it was crowded with two of us inside. But we had a 180 degree view of the forest around us, the leafless trees standing tall like rows of endless toothpicks.

I rested my gun on the window and slid my back against the wall.

"I'm sorry for last night," Elizabeth said.

I tensed. The kiss? "You don't have to apologize."

"Sure I do," she insisted. "I was upset about possibly being stuck out here for a week or longer. I understand you're only trying to keep me safe."

Oh. She didn't mean the kiss. "I would be frustrated too if I were in your shoes," was all I said.

"The thing you have to understand," Elizabeth began, "is that you being assigned to me was a political decision. POTUS suspected I was going to announce my candidacy, so he gave me a Secret Service detail to make me seem weaker. Like I need protecting."

I grunted. I hadn't thought of it from her angle. I'd been too focused on why I had been assigned to her. My own personal fuck-up.

"You said it yourself," she went on. "This order came from the top. Right?"

"It did."

"Surely you can see how keeping me hidden away for a week damages my political clout. A senator announces that she's running for president, then disappears for a week? It gives POTUS the ammunition to hammer me for being scared. He'll claim that if I can't handle the heat of the first day of my official campaign, I won't be able to handle the *actual* presidency."

"I hadn't thought of it like that," I admitted.

"It's not your job to think of that," she said gently. "It's your job to keep me safe. Which you're absolutely dedicated to. I can see that now. But we can't keep me so safe that I can't do what I was elected to do. A ship is safe in harbor, but that is not what ships are built for."

"What would you have me do?" I asked. "My orders are to keep you here, with limited communication, until told otherwise. Should I disobey those and let you run back home to your campaign?"

She sighed. "I don't know what to do, Luca. I just want you to understand where my frustration comes from. I'm not used to any of this."

She put her hand on my leg, and I instinctively reached out to clasp it. I gave it a squeeze and said, "I understand your frustration, Elizabeth."

We shared a smile in the cramped deer blind. She had the deepest, widest eyes I'd ever seen. A man could drown in those eyes if he stared too long. Already I could feel my hesitation disappearing, the urge to cup her cheek and kiss her growing with every second our hands kept touching.

Her head whipped around. "What's that?"

I pulled out my binoculars. A single deer moved between the trees in the distance. A doe by herself.

"Good eyes," I said, swapping my binoculars for

my rifle. I gazed through the scope and centered the crosshairs on the doe. I took a steady breath, then exhaled and prepared to squeeze the trigger.

Elizabeth's rifle fired, causing me to flinch and almost drop my gun. With expert speed she pulled back the bolt to discharge the shell, pushed it back forward to load a new round, and fired a second time. I looked through the scope and saw the doe on the ground.

"Sorry," she said with a sigh. "Should've gotten her on the first shot. I'm rusty."

I stared at her. "You said you've never hunted before!"

"I'm a politician," she said with a shit-eating grin. "And politician's lie. Come on. Let's go grab our supper and check the rest of the perimeter. I'm freezing my butt off."

I watched her climb down the blind with newfound respect.

28

Elizabeth

Luca carried the doe across his shoulders while I held both rifles. Obviously it left us a little more vulnerable since it would take him longer to get a weapon out, but we didn't have much of a choice.

"I grew up hunting," I explained as we walked. It still wasn't warm out, but now that the sun was above the trees and shining on our backs it was close to pleasant. "I wasn't big into killing living things, but dad insisted on teaching me. He said it was part of our culture."

"You didn't hesitate on this doe," Luca said with a grin.

"Because we intend to actually eat it. It's not just killing for sport."

"You don't *have* to eat it, though."

I snickered. "I saw what was in the cupboards. I can't survive off freeze dried mashed potatoes and boiled rice, whether for two days or two weeks."

Boomer barked once as if to agree.

"While we're on the subject of killing, who would want to kill *you*?"

"Same as I told the officers after my first attack. I'm a politician from a swing state. Half the country probably wants me dead."

"Do you think it has anything to do with your candidacy?"

"I don't see why. I hadn't even announced yet when I was attacked on my jog."

"But did anyone know you were *planning* on running for president?"

I thought about it for a moment. "Just my campaign manager. But there were plenty of rumors and speculation, both from inside our party and outside." I paused. "We *did* hire a company to run a thorough background check on me. They probably put the pieces together. Maybe sold that information to someone else."

"Huh," Luca grunted. He'd shouldered the weight of the doe easily, and still showed no sign of getting tired on our march back to the cabin. "Do you think you have a chance of beating Bob Pollock in the primary?"

"I doubt I'll beat *any* of the other candidates, whether that's Senator Pollock or someone else. I'm really not much of a threat," I admitted. "I just turned 35. I have far less experience than the rest of the field. Honestly, we're just angling for a VP spot on someone else's ticket. Why would anyone kill me over that?"

"Another VP hopeful?"

"Seems like a lot of effort to fight over second place," I said.

"That banker," Luca suddenly said. "The one you grilled in the Finance Committee the other day. He stormed out of there like his tail was on fire. That's someone pissed off enough to try to get even."

"His testimony in front of our committee was *after* I was first attacked," I pointed out. "But I like your line of thinking. There are plenty of corporations we go after on the Finance Committee. Lots of corruption."

"You'd think they could do a better job," Luca muttered.

I looked sideways at him as we climbed over a fallen tree. "What do you mean?"

"I don't know." He was silent for a few steps. "I don't want to alarm you."

"I can handle the blunt truth," I said.

"Pussyfooting around it only pisses me off."

He hesitated, like he didn't want to say it. Finally he sighed and looked over at me.

"You were a sitting duck up there on the Ohio Statehouse steps," he said. "You stood behind the podium, without moving, for several minutes. The shooter had plenty of time to take a clean shot. Any mediocre assassin could have picked you off with ease."

I shivered. "You're right. That *does* alarm me." I paused. "The balloons probably obscured the shot."

"Right. Why wait until then to take the shot? The shooter must have only gotten into position at the end of your speech."

I looked at him. "Does that help us narrow down who did it?"

"No," he sighed. "Not really."

Or maybe they wanted to wait until I announced my candidacy. I dismissed the thought outright. If someone wanted to kill me, it shouldn't have mattered if I was a candidate or not.

"There we go," Luca said as the cabin came into view. "My shoulders are killing me."

I grinned at the admission as we went inside.

*

Without much else to do, I curled up on the couch and pulled up the same book I'd been reading on my eReader for the past 6 months, a few pages at a time. Luca positioned the doe on a table outside and set to cleaning it for the next hour.

I thought about our kiss last night. Clearly, it had been a mistake. An impulsive move by me, and a moment of weakness for him. The way he'd avoided physical contact since then showed that he didn't have feelings for me, physical or otherwise.

Stupid Elizabeth. You've already slept with Ethan and Anthony. Now you're trying to make it three-of-a-kind?

Yet I couldn't help but glance out the window at my strapping Secret Service detail. Especially when he finished cleaning the deer, grabbed an axe, and started splitting logs for firewood on an old tree stump. After a minute of work he stripped off his jacket and shirt until he was wearing only a white wifebeater and jeans. His corded muscles rippled in the sunlight as he raised the axe over his head and brought it down, again and again in the frigid cold. The exercise warmed his body to the point that steam rose off his skin, making him look like some mythological creature of mist.

When he was done, he rested the axe behind his head with both hands and stretched. The suit he wore on most days did a good job of hiding how *ripped* he was. Luca wasn't a guy who got chiseled in the gym. Those muscles were from manual labor.

He turned around and glanced at me through the window. I quickly returned my eyes to my book and hoped he didn't realize how long I'd been staring.

Luca got a fire going in his smoker and then cut hunks of meat off the doe carcass. Boomer sat on his haunches nearby until Luca tossed him a few strips of meat, which the loyal dog chomped on and swallowed quickly. Once the smoker was going he pulled out a vacuum-seal contraption to store the rest of the meat. By the time he was done he had dozens of packages of meat stacked on the table.

"Doing okay in here?" he asked as he came inside and began storing them in the freezer.

"Yep," I said. "Need any help?"

He turned away from the fridge. His muscular arms hung out of his wifebeater, glistening with sweat despite the frigid temperature outside. "Nah, I've got it. You haven't tried to escape yet?"

"Not yet. I'm still working out the logistics of my getaway."

He poured himself a glass of water and gulped it down. "If you try to make a break for it on foot, be sure to pack warm. I'll definitely lose my job if you freeze to death in the middle of the forest."

"I'll take that under consideration."

He smiled as he went back outside.

In stark contrast to my days on the Hill which flew by, the day in the cabin *crawled*. I tried to force myself to relax and enjoy my book, but it was impossible to turn off the part of my brain that was churning a mile a minute. Thinking of campaign events, poll results, and media reaction to my candidacy. I'd spent my entire life dreaming about running for president! Now that I was officially running, it was torture to not even be involved.

Luca didn't seem to mind. He busied himself with tasks around the cabin. Starting a fire in the huge brick fireplace, then stacking enough logs next to it to keep it running for months. Next he went into the kitchen and took inventory of all the dry goods: sacks of beans, freeze-dried mashed potatoes, pasta, and rice. He rearranged it until he was satisfied and then set out to cleaning the dust off the cupboards.

I lasted until late afternoon before tossing my book aside. "I'm going nuts. Can I use your Wi-Fi hotspot again?"

He poked his head up from a cabinet. "If you promise not to login to any of your email accounts. If whoever wants to kill you is tracking your accounts, the IP address might lead them right to us."

"I promise," I said as I moved to the table with my laptop.

But as I sat down, I positioned myself so that Luca couldn't see my screen from the kitchen.

I spent an hour checking all the news sites. Now that a day had passed, op-eds had gone out in most of the major publications around the country. The good news? Most of the reaction to my candidacy was positive. Some *very* positive. The editor for the Columbus Star said the attempt on my life, "...proves that Senator O'Hare is a candidate to be reckoned with, who threatens the status-quo." There were dozens more like that. I had to search hard for a negative opinion about my campaign. That came from the editor of a small North Carolina paper who claimed the assassination attempt was a *false flag attack*—that is, a fake attack orchestrated by me personally!—to generate sympathy for my campaign. I rolled my eyes so hard I might have given myself astigmatism.

One thing was playing especially well in the media: my initial reaction to the shooting. While the bullets flew toward me I held my ground, staring defiantly out at the shooter until my Secret Service Agent covered me and escorted me off the stage. Little did they know I thought the gunshots were coming from the confetti cannons.

I glanced at Luca. He was still on his hands and knees cleaning the lower cabinets in the kitchen.

I opened Chrome in Incognito Mode so it wouldn't record my history, then logged into my personal email account.

924 new emails in the last day. Goodness gracious.

I searched for Megan's email address and found a dozen emails from her. I skimmed the first few lines of each email to get a feel for what she was saying:

Elizabeth! I've been praying you're safe, but they won't tell me where they've taken you. Some unspecified secure location...

Elizabeth, the press is eating this up! As tragic as it was, I can spin it. Don't make any public statements before talking to me first. If Special Agent Tightpants will even let you...

Elizabeth, it's very important that you call me AS SOON AS POSSIBLE. The longer you're gone, the more suspicious people are getting. They need to see your face. People are starting to talk...

Elizabeth. They can't just kidnap and whisk you away without consulting me. I've canceled all the campaign stops we had scheduled for Ohio. Which sucks, since I called in a lot of favors to line some of them up...

Elizabeth! This isn't funny anymore. Call me ASAP.

Elizabeth, we're losing all of our momentum here. I don't care if you have to crawl away from your detail on your hands and knees. Come back to civilization!

I quickly sent her a new email telling her I was safe, and not to do anything drastic.

"Wine?"

I flinched as Luca held up a bottle of wine in the kitchen. It was covered with so much dust that the label was just a grey splotch.

"I can't promise it's any good," he said, "but it's the only booze we have."

"You're going to drink on the job?" I asked with surprise.

"The offer was just for you," he said coolly. "Want a glass with dinner?"

I sighed. "I'll take a glass right now, and then *another* with dinner."

He came over to the table so quickly that I had to scramble to close my email.

"What's the world saying about the candidacy of Senator Elizabeth O'Hare?" he asked while opening the wine next to me.

I spun the laptop around so he could see. "The New York Times is calling me a hero."

He snorted. "Hero, huh?"

"Right?" I replied with an incredulous laugh. "I heroically stood on stage while ignoring what I thought were the popping sounds from the confetti cannons. Nevermind that the *real* hero was the man who shielded me with his body and ushered me to safety."

"Nothing heroic about that," he said. "I did what any other agent would do. By the way, Ethan did a fantastic job."

"Oh, right! I forgot all about him! Did you ever find out who he tackled? Was it an accomplice of the shooter?"

Luca grimaced. "No such luck. The guy was totally unrelated. Some Capitol Policeman watching your speech."

I froze. "A Capitol Policeman?"

"It makes as little sense to me too," he said. "No idea why he was all the way out in Ohio, though. Must've been on vacation or something. All I know is they cleared him."

Anthony. He'd been watching from the crowd. And Ethan noticed him and tackled him.

I'd totally forgotten about my other two protectors. I had too much else on my mind. If Megan was losing her mind trying to contact me, both of them were probably *really* worried.

I accepted the glass of wine from Luca and drank deeply. The wine wasn't good. In fact, it was pretty terrible. But it was better than nothing.

"Still, that was good work from your bodyguard," Luca said. "He's got sharp eyes. I don't know what you're paying him, but he's worth every penny."

I'll say.

Luca sat in the chair next to me. His skin was tight with corded muscle, with a smattering of freckles on his shoulders and forearms. The muscles in his arm bulged as he ran a hand through his hair and looked around the cabin. "Feels good to clean this place up. Lot of good memories here."

"Memories with your ex-wife?"

"Hah! Not really."

He didn't elaborate.

"Why didn't you two work out?" I asked. "Or is it complicated?"

He smiled sadly. "It's actually very simple. She hated D.C., and I didn't want to leave my job. Every time we came back home she got all gloomy and talked about how she wished we could move back permanently. In the end, it was too much for both of us."

"Ah."

"I couldn't go back to the simple life," he said. "Getting a regular nine-to-five job in a small Kentucky town? I couldn't do that. Not after spending almost two decades protecting the most powerful people in America."

"I'm sorry."

"Don't be. Carey understood why I couldn't leave, and I understood why she couldn't stay. It wasn't meant to be."

"Do you believe in that?" I asked, feeling philosophical. "That things are *meant to be*? That everything happens for a reason?"

He frowned in thought. Small wrinkles appeared at the corners of his eyes. They didn't make him look old, though. Only experienced. A man who knew who he was, and what he wanted in life.

"I suppose I do," he said. "Much of my life was random events. Catching the eye of a Louisville scout one day in high school practice, which got me a full ride. My professor encouraging me to apply to the Secret Service. I can think of a dozen little things like that which steered me toward where I am in life. It's difficult to imagine any of that happening by chance alone." He glanced at me. "You probably think that's dumb."

"No, not at all."

"But I can tell you don't believe it yourself."

I gave him an apologetic grimace. "I don't. Sorry. Not that I think less of you for believing it!"

"Everyone's different," he said simply. "What's your take on all this?" His gesture encompassed more than just the cabin. He was talking about the world. Life in general.

I thought very carefully before answering. I

didn't want to offend him.

"Everything I've gotten in life, I had to work hard for," I explained. "My high school teachers discouraged me from pursuing political science, so I had to spend twice as much time on my papers to get them to take me seriously. College was much the same. I had to search high and low for a campaign manager who would take a chance on a rookie city council member, and then when I *did* find Megan Hanram I spent weeks actually convincing her to work for me. Every campaign I've ever run, whether at the state or national level, I've worked twice as hard as my opponents. Not to throw out the gender card, but women have to spend twice as long on their appearance than men. Daily exercise is mandatory for someone like me, because although a male politician can be overweight and still be taken seriously, being overweight is the kiss of death for a female politician. That's the shitty reality. But rather than let it discourage me, I pushed through it and worked my ass off every single day to get where I am."

Luca nodded along. "Were there no random bits of luck along the way? No chance encounters that changed your career?"

"Maybe some. Meeting Megan right after she'd been fired from her previous campaign was lucky. But overall, my career is defined by the hard work I have put in. Not by luck along the way. If that makes sense."

"It does," Luca said. "You've definitely worked

hard to get where you are. It shows."

He looked away, as if embarrassed by what he'd said. Or *scared* of what thoughts were going on behind those sharp eyes.

"Even though you don't want to leave Washington," I said, "you seem to enjoy the simple life. Hunting. Chopping wood. It suits you."

He shrugged one shoulder. "I enjoy it. But it's not my purpose. I'd get sick of all this after a week or two." He sighed deeply. "I don't know *what* I'll do when I retire."

I sipped my wine. It wasn't so bad once you drank enough of it. "You won't have to worry about that for a while, right?"

"Actually, most agents retire before age 40," he said. "Only the most elite are kept longer. Which I thought I was... Until I got on someone's bad side." He stared off. "I'm scared they're going to force me into retirement as soon as your assignment is over, no matter how well I do."

I reached out and took his hand. "I'm really sorry, Luca. If it helps, I'll give you a glowing review."

A moment passed between us. Like a jolt of electricity through our hands, fusing them together. Leaving everything all tingly.

He pulled his hand away awkwardly. "Elizabeth..."

"Who knows," I said, trying to quickly change

the subject. "If I become vice president I can request you personally. Call in some favors."

He wasn't easily distracted. His eyes bore into mine. "Elizabeth. About what happened last night."

Damnit. I'd pushed too hard. I was such an idiot. He didn't have feelings for me. Because why would he? We'd only known each other for a few days. A lot had happened in that time, but still.

Yet I'd pushed my luck anyways.

"It's perfectly normal to feel... attraction to someone after a traumatic event," he said. "It's the typical human response. The brain attaching itself to whatever is near."

I listened to his speech and sipped more bad wine. I'd screwed things up, and now it was awkward and uncomfortable.

"That's why we can't act on our feelings," he said. He wasn't looking at me now. Like he was afraid to. "We have to resist whatever urges we may have."

"What?" I said. "*We?*"

"You're a senator. Hell, you're a presidential candidate now. And I'm a Secret Service agent. It would be disastrous for both of us to make a rash decision. We would both regret it later."

We. He kept saying *we.* He had feelings for me too. Urges.

It was impossible to look at him as just another

guy, a platonic robot at my side for these past few days. Luca Santos was a handsome, ripped man who had *saved my life*. He'd shielded me with his body, and then carried me in his arms to safety.

He was my hero.

"We can't lose sight of what really matters," he finished. "We're both too career-driven to risk something stupid."

I finished the wine in one gulp and put the glass down. I rose from my chair, threw one leg over his body, and lowered myself onto his lap.

"Fuck our careers."

29

Elizabeth

A hundred different emotions ran through Luca's eyes as I straddled him on the chair and wrapped my arms around his neck. Surprise. Excitement. A little fear.

But beneath it all I could see the lust, burning brighter with every passing second. A lust which couldn't be denied.

"Elizabeth," he said.

"Fuck our careers," I repeated. "I could be assassinated next week. And you're going to lose your job no matter what happens. You might as well enjoy yourself before it ends."

The fire in his eyes grew wider.

I leaned in slowly, devouring the way he watched me with rising excitement. He *ached* for me, I could tell. The look in his eyes didn't match his words.

And I wanted him just as badly.

The kiss was a firework exploding in my sex. His hands ran up my legs and gripped my plump ass, holding me down against his now throbbing hard-on. Like a giant awakening from slumber his appetite rose and unfolded itself, kissing me hard and squeezing me tighter breathing faster while thrusting up against my sex. I imagined that each phantom thrust was his cock pushing deeper inside me. I pushed down against him hard, desperate to feel his touch.

He rose from the chair, lifting me with ease. He carried me across the cabin to the fireplace, lowering me down to the old bear-skin rug. It was soft against my back as he smothered me with his body, taking care not to press against my bandage.

"I've wanted you," I whispered as he kissed me again.

"I've wanted you so badly it's been *painful*," he said. "A deep ache in my soul…"

I reached between us and took hold of his throbbing hard-on. "Deep in your *soul*, huh?"

He grinned. "There too."

We had our clothes off quickly, and although he tried to slide his mouth down between my legs I wanted him too badly to waste any time on foreplay. I grabbed his ass and pulled him into me, and we both exhaled like we were dying as he slid all the way in.

We kissed slowly and passionately while making love on the rug, and all the while Luca wrapped his arms around me and held me close, the same way he'd protected me on the steps of the Ohio Statehouse, and since we were in the middle of nowhere we could scream our screams of ecstasy as loud as we wanted in the cabin.

*

The fire crackled next to us, giving off pulsing heat that alternated between too hot and too weak. It needed another log or two. It would only take a few seconds.

But neither of us wanted to leave the floor.

"That..." Luca said. His mouth was in my hair, a deep buzz. "That was incredible."

"Mmm hmm," I said happily. "You're the best Secret Service agent I've ever had."

"I'm the only one you've ever had."

"Details, details."

"I'm afraid you're going to regret it later," he said carefully. "I would never tell anyone about what happened, but these things have a way of getting out."

"You're *really* ruining the perfect mood."

"Think of your campaign."

I nuzzled against his neck and sighed. "I've done nothing but think about my presidential campaign since I was a teenager watching the Bush-Gore debates on television with my parents. I've missed out on a lot of life because I've been too focused on my political ambitions. It feels good to do something like this." I looked up into his eyes. "Even if someday we'll look back and think it's a mistake."

He grunted. I felt it through my whole body since I was laying half on his chest. "I won't think it's a mistake. Like you said, my career at the Service is probably over no matter what happens. But you have a bright political future. I'd hate to be the person to fuck all that up."

"You won't be," I said. I thought of Ethan, and Anthony before him. Several lovers all within a short span of time. The logical part of my brain knew they were *all* mistakes.

The rest of my brain didn't care.

"Want to know the truth?" I asked.

"Always."

I felt like I could be honest with Luca. Vulnerable. So the words came pouring out. "I'm terrified of the future. I'm terrified of the potential responsibility I may take on. Running for president is all I've ever wanted, and now that it's here I'm terrified of *failing*. Did you know that I've never lost an election? Going all the way back to my first run at City Council. I've never lost. But now I'm entering a race that I have no chance of winning. No *intention* of winning."

"Then why do it?" Luca asked. "I mean, aside from trying to grab a VP spot."

"I don't know," I replied. "Because it's the next step forward. Because it's a good plan to become president in eight years." I laughed. "Because Megan talked me into it."

"You can't launch a presidential campaign just because someone else says it's a good idea."

I sat up and ran a caressing hand across his bare chest. He had a small tuft of sandy-colored chest hair between his pecs. "But the reasoning holds up! Eight years as veep would give me a leg up on the election I *do* intend to win. It's the smart move, even if my heart isn't in it completely."

"You know what isn't the smart move? Making love to your devastatingly handsome Secret Service Agent on the floor of his log cabin." He put his hands behind his head as a pillow and grinned widely. On the agent's normally serious face, it looked adorable.

I poked him it the belly. "I know. But that's kind of my point. Maybe, deep down, I'm trying to sabotage my own campaign before it begins."

"Ahh, the subconscious. Sabotaging careers

since mankind walked upright." Luca scrunched his face up. "There might be something to that. I'm not a psychologist by any stretch, but I bet a psychologist would agree with your diagnosis. But you know what?"

"What?"

He rose to a sitting position and cupped my cheek. "I'm glad your subconscious made this mistake."

"Me too."

He kissed me softly, then jumped up. "My subconscious is telling me that I'm starving. So is my conscious, and every other part of my body."

"Me too!"

We put our clothes back on and Luca retrieved the venison from the smoker. He cooked a can of green beans in a skillet with butter and served that up with the meat onto two large plates. Then he emptied the rest of the bottle of wine into two glasses.

"I thought you couldn't drink on the job," I teased.

He brought the glasses over to the table. "Yeah, well, I'm not supposed to have sex with the people I'm protecting, either. So it's a night of firsts."

I accepted the glass and raised it high. "To breaking rules."

He clinked his glass to mine and drank. "Good lord. That's *awful*. How did you drink an entire glass of this already?"

"With willpower alone."

Both of us went silent while we ate. The venison had a wonderful smoky flavor, and was perfectly juicy on the inside. It reminded me of my dad serving freshly hunted meat at our own dinner table. Delicious and nostalgic at the same time.

"So," Luca said when his plate was almost empty. "We know there are a lot of people who could possibly want you dead."

"Sleeping with you was supposed to be a *distraction* from my assassination attempts," I said.

"Well, I've been thinking about it." He stabbed another piece of meat with his fork and pointed it at me. "And I just can't understand how an assassin could be so bad at their job. The first attack outside your apartment. He was directly ahead of you? And you were running straight toward him?"

"Right."

"And the report said you were something like 30 feet away when he fired his gun?"

"30 or 40," I agreed.

"And you didn't react until the first gunshot?"

"Correct."

Luca bit into the piece of meat and then stared at the fork. "A target coming straight at them, well illuminated by the street lamps. That should have been an easy shot for anyone, let alone a trained assassin. It would have been impossible to miss."

"What are you thinking?" I asked. "The assassin missed on purpose?"

"I don't know," Luca said. I could tell he was deep in thought. "Maybe it's not really an assassin. It could be some random nutjob. You're a good-looking woman. *Great*-looking," he quickly added after I glared at him. "Maybe they're a stalker. Someone who wants to scare you, but doesn't want to actually kill you."

"I guess," I said. "But that doesn't make me feel any better. If it was some big conspiracy by another politician or that bank CEO or some other lobbying group, we can track that down and uncover it. It's a lot tougher to find one psychopathic stalker."

"Sometimes life works out that way," he admitted. "At least you're safe out here in the middle of nowhere with me." He flashed me a smile.

It was comforting... but only for a moment. *Ships are safe in harbor...*

"Luca," I said gently. "You know I can't stay here forever."

"I know."

"I can't even stay here for another day or two."

"I know."

"I have to go back to Washington."

"I know," he repeated. "But I have my orders to keep you here."

"So is that it? I'm a prisoner?"

He chuckled. "The DHS Secretary, who has total oversight of the Service, has a surprising amount of power when it comes to national security."

I sighed to myself. I wanted to blame him, but it wasn't his fault. He was just following orders. And as much as I wanted to convince him to let me go, if anything happened to me because of that he would never forgive himself. That would *truly* ruin his career. It would destroy him as a person.

I couldn't do that to him. I'd have to be patient.

"What would you do if I opened the door and tried to walk out right now?" I asked.

"I'd have to stop you."

"I would just try again," I said, allowing a little bit of mischief to trickle into my tone. "And again. And again after that."

He smiled, then coughed and made his face into a mask of seriousness. The way a Secret Service Agent was *supposed* to look. "Well, then. I might have to restrain you, ma'am."

I leaned forward. "I'm listening."

He scrunched his face in mock thought. "Well, I would probably tie you to the bed. It's up against that wall, away from most of the windows. The safest place."

"Makes sense," I said. "I didn't think you had any handcuffs, though."

"Who needs handcuffs?" he said. "I have plenty of other things to tie you down."

30

Elizabeth

We stared at each other for a long moment.

I jumped up from the table and sprinted for the front door. Luca was on me faster than I expected, wrapping his arms around me from behind so tight I couldn't move. I tried not to giggle. It would ruin the fun.

He threw me over his shoulder, giving me a top-down view of his chiseled ass. I gave one cheek a smack, then the other.

"Cut it out," he said.

"Make me."

He used his free hand to smack my own ass, *hard*. A shiver of pleasure ran through my body.

"I can smack your ass too. And I'm stronger."

He tossed me on the bed. I bounced up and down and crossed my legs while waiting to see what he would do. The completely nude agent stood in front of me like a statue chiseled from marble, his upper half shaped like a wonderful V of muscle.

"Don't go anywhere," he warned.

Without dressing, he went outside. Across the room, Boomer lifted his head off the couch, made a happy noise, and laid back down. Luca returned a minute later with a long coil of metal in his hands. "No rope. This'll have to do."

He extended two feet of steel chain and held it taut in front of him with two fists. I felt a tingle of excitement as he grinned at me.

I pretended to resist as he held me down and tied my hands with the chains, looping them around my wrist, around one corner of the bed frame, then the other, then back down to tie my other wrist.

I tested the movement in my arms. I could lower one hand toward my head, but as soon as I did the chain pulled my other hand farther toward the bedpost. As a result I could barely do anything.

Luca loomed over me, examining his handiwork. "It'll do," he said, then disappeared into the kitchen.

"Hey," I said. "Where are you going?" I tried to lean forward but couldn't see him around the curve of the refrigerator.

"You'll see."

I shivered on the bed. I was totally vulnerable. If he was a psychopath he could have done whatever he wanted with me. But since I knew I could trust him...

I heard the soft pop of a cork, and then my nude guardian returned with another dusty bottle of wine. He took a long pull from it and made a face. "That's as nasty as the first bottle."

He stretched his arms wide and arched his back, giving me a long look at his body. The more I saw of him, the more I wanted.

"What are you going to do to me?" I asked in a soft voice.

"Haven't decided yet." He knelt on the bed next to my legs and tipped the bottle. "But this is what I'm going to do first."

I yelped as a trickle of red wine hit my breasts and ran down my belly. "You're staining the sheets!" I said.

"It's worth it for the fun I'm going to have with you."

He set the bottle down on the side table and then bent over my face for a kiss. I closed my eyes and prepared my lips, but it never came. When I opened them again, Luca was two inches away, grinning.

"You're an eager beaver," he said in a sensual whisper.

"I have a gorgeous Secret Service agent nude above me," I purred. "Can you blame me?"

"What I can do is *this*."

He lowered his lips to my neck and kissed the wine from my skin. Another shiver ran through my body as he sucked gently, tasting the wine. "It's far more delicious this way," he said.

"Oh?" I breathed.

He responded by sucking some more wine out of the gap in my collarbone, then along my breast. I squirmed on the bed as he made his way along my chest, kissing and tasting the wine like I was a human wine glass. The hairs on his arm tickled my porcelain skin.

He grabbed the bottle and let out another trickle, this time lower, but on the side opposite my bandage. It slid along my hip and down around my ass cheek, collecting on the sheets he no longer cared about. Now his lips drank what was in my belly button, then the parts along my pelvic bone, then a light kiss at the edge of my mound of pubic hair.

"How's it taste?" I asked.

He grinned up at me. "The wine's much tastier this way."

"I'd like to return the favor."

He waggled a finger at me. "This is my fun."

Luca grabbed the wine and poured a final trickle down my belly. The cool liquid collected in my mound and trickled down my labia. I held my breath as he placed the bottle on the table and lowered himself to me.

His first kiss was soft, but the anticipation had my swollen sex aching for his touch. I moaned the moment his lips pressed against my thigh, close enough that his cheek brushed against my sex. For the next minute he did everything *but* kiss my private parts: he went all around it in a slow circle, his breath hot and his cheek scratchy from this morning's shave. I arched my back and moaned and did everything I could to beg him to taste *me*, but he resisted with the willpower of a monk.

And then, without warning, he gave in.

His tongue licked from the bottom of my pussy up my lips to my clit. The noises and squirms I made were unflattering but I was too lost in his touch to be embarrassed.

"*You* taste much better than the wine."

I didn't have time to say anything witty in response because he was burying his tongue deep into my pussy, *impossibly* deep, there was no way a man could have a tongue this long, it was like a snake writhing against my inner walls! I yearned to grab hold of his close-cropped hair and hold him to my sex but the chains caught tight and restrained me.

Somehow, that made everything a thousand times hotter. My lack of control. It was like being in those hotel rooms with Ethan, but dialed up to 11.

Unable to do anything, I accepted Luca's cunning cunnilingus like the good guest that I was. In and out his tongue went, fucking me like a rigid penis, then swirling and bucking inside of me like a mad scientist's machine made for pleasure. And when my breath drew short and the explosion in my sex could not be withheld, I squeezed my thighs around his head and held him close while crying out my pleasure to the wooden ceiling beams.

"Mrph hrmph."

"Oh, sorry," I said, loosening my thigh-grip on his head. He came up red-faced, but grinning.

"You seemed to enjoy that as much as I did."

I scoffed. "There's no way you enjoyed that more than I did."

"I love pleasing a beautiful woman," he said as he caressed my thighs.

"*You* should be the escort," I said absently.

"What?"

I gave a start. "You should be *an* escort. For money. I know a lot of women who would pay top dollar for that kind of treatment."

He rested his head against my belly. "Doing it for money would probably ruin the fun."

"You're probably right." I stretched my back, hands still restrained above me. "As fun as that was, now I'm all sticky with wine residue."

I felt his lips pull into a grin. "Then we'd better get you into the bath."

31

Elizabeth

By the time the tub was filled with water, the entire bathroom was steaming like a sauna. Luca finally unchained me and insisted on carrying me to the bathroom like a wounded animal, which I suppose I kind of was.

"I have this," I said, tapping my bandage. "Can it get wet?"

He lowered me to my feet and removed the bandage. I winced as the cloth pulled against my wound, then finally peeled free. A square of pale white skin surrounded the gash, which was about an inch long and held closed with stitches. The skin underneath the stitching was purple and swollen.

"*That's* attractive," I muttered, feeling a tingle of self-consciousness even though I was totally nude and had just had Luca's face between my legs.

He dragged his fingertips across the wound in a loving caress. "I think you're beautiful," he said, kissing me softly on the cheek. "*Because* you're strong enough to survive an assassination attempt, not in spite of it." His fingers tapped on the wound. "This will eventually scar over, but don't ever let it feel like a weakness. This is proof you can withstand anything life throws at you."

"I hadn't thought about it that way." I touched the wound tentatively. "Is it safe for the water?"

"Pretty sure it is. I'll reapply the bandages later."

"My hero." I kissed him on the lips and then stepped into the tub. The water was so hot it made my toes tingle. I had to stand knee-deep in it for several seconds before lowering myself down a few inches at a time. Finally I gripped the edges and lowered my upper body underneath the surface, sighing as the soothing heat spread through my body.

"Oh, that's *nice.*"

Luca sank into the other side of the tub, stretching out his legs. His toes poked against my thigh.

We closed our eyes and enjoyed the soothing water, too relaxed to speak.

Sometime later Luca said, "Something just occurred to me."

I opened one eye. "What's that?"

His head was still craned back and his eyes were closed. "I left my sidearm in the other room. If anyone knocked the door down..."

"Boomer will protect us," I said. "Won't you, boy?"

At the sound of his name, the black lab came trotting into the bathroom. I squealed as he licked my face and neck.

Luca leaned forward in the tub. "No! Don't go just yet."

He wrapped his arms around me and scooted toward my half of the tub. "I wasn't."

He pulled me forward until my legs were wrapped around him and my chest was pressed wetly against his. "Hi," I said.

"Oh, hello."

"I hate to spoil the mood," I said, "but bath sex isn't as sexy as it sounds."

He smiled knowingly. "Water isn't a lubricant. I've made that mistake before." He cupped a handful of water and sloughed it over my back. "I just wanted to hold you close. Get the sticky wine off you."

"Mmm," I hummed. "I retract my previous objection. Carry on."

I closed my eyes and enjoyed my Secret Service agent holding me close and rubbing me down with slow, loving strokes.

*

The next two days were wonderfully carefree. I stopped checking my email because I was getting tired of Megan's frantic insistence. Luca and I ate smoked venison, and we made love, and we hiked in the woods like two lovers on their honeymoon, hand-in-hand.

I stopped caring about the stresses of Washington. Of my campaign. Of the man—or men—who wanted to kill me. Those could all wait until *this* was over. This perfect wooded getaway with a man whose job it was to protect my life.

And then, one day, everything fell apart.

32

Elizabeth

We were out for an after-dinner hike along one of the many game trails in the forest. The chill in the air intensified as the sun dropped below the tree line, but that also gave us a gorgeous painting of a sunset spreading across the clouds, orange and pink and purple as far as the eye could see.

It was beautiful out here. It made me miss home a little bit.

Boomer suddenly shot away into the woods after a squirrel. Both of us laughed. "I thought we'd never be alone," Luca said.

"What do you mean?"

He turned and pushed me against a tree, kissing me forcefully. His tongue was warm and soft as it wedged its way into my mouth to swirl with my own, and his hand pried open my legs. I moaned as he rubbed me through my jeans there in the forest.

Luca pulled away with a sigh, eyes boring into mine with happiness. "What was that for?" I asked.

"I just really wanted to kiss you, is all."

A giggle escaped my lips. "I bet you say that to all your assignments."

"Just the ones I want to take back to my cabin and ravage."

"Ohh. That sounds like fun. Break out the chains again?"

"Only if you're a naughty girl."

"Naughty *senator*," I corrected. "Show some respect."

We held hands and continued on our hike.

"Let's assume the worst," I said.

Luca frowned at me. "I don't like this change in conversation at all."

"Let's say you *do* get forced into retirement after this assignment," I said. "What kind of alternative careers do you have lined up?"

"None," he said, resigned. "There's nothing else I would like to do. I'm open to suggestions."

I gave him a long, appraising look. "You'd make a good lumberjack."

"Hah!"

I ticked off points on my fingers. "You look good in plaid. You like the outdoors. And you look *very* sexy swinging an axe."

"You were watching me chop wood the other day?"

"How could I not? That was hotter than porn."

He smiled to himself. "I'll take it under consideration. What else do you have?"

"All joking aside, the obvious answer is private security. A bodyguard. I bet some big Hollywood stars or other New York celebrities would pay a lot of money to hire a former Secret Service Agent as their bodyguard. Your life and job would hardly change at all."

"I'm skeptical that protecting a teen pop star would be as fulfilling as protecting the leader of the free world. But that's not a bad idea."

"Or you could actually retire," I said. "I don't know what your financial situation is, but you could live out here. Hunting and fishing and chopping wood to your heart's content."

He shook his head. "These are the kinds of things I like to do for just a few days. I'd go nuts after a week. I need something *real* to do."

CRACK-POW came the sound of a gunshot

behind us.

There was a thudding sound, and Luca cried out. He dropped to his hands and knees and groaned.

"No!" I said, falling to my knees beside him. "Are you okay?" There was a little fabric bag on the ground behind him. Tan, like a tea bag.

He fell to his side and rolled over. Pain was painted on his face as he reached for his sidearm. "Elizabeth... Run..."

Leaves rattled. I turned my head to see a man sprinting through the trees toward us. A black ski mask covered his face, and he held a shotgun in his hand.

I raised my rifle, but a second man was suddenly at my side, grabbing the rifle and wrenching it from my hands. He stepped over me and kicked Luca's pistol. It bounced along the hard ground and came to a stop 10 feet away.

"No!" I screamed, full of fear and panic and dread. "Please don't kill me, I'll do anything..."

"Elizabeth!" Luca roared, cutting off as the other man wrapped duct tape around his mouth. He rolled Luca over and then tied his hands behind his back.

"Leave him alone!" I shouted. "Please don't hurt us..."

I kicked and fought and punched at my assailants, but it was like striking two brick walls. They carried me like a sack of grain between them up the game trail. Luca's muffled cries faded behind us.

A rusted Jetta was parked next to Luca's rental car at the cabin. They opened the back seat and shoved me inside. One of them joined me in the back while the other climbed into the driver seat. Gravel flew as the car peeled out of there.

"You're going to go to jail for the rest of your lives," I said. My heartbeat was a pounding drum in my ears. "Kidnapping a senator... *killing* a senator..."

The man next to me smiled behind his ski mask. "Hey there, sugar."

I squinted. "*Anthony?*"

He pulled off the ski mask. His dark hair was a mess but he had a huge grin on his face. "Miss me?"

The driver pulled his mask off. Familiar green eyes glanced at me in the rear-view mirror. "Sorry about all this, Elizabeth. Figured you wouldn't mind once you knew it was us."

"What... What the hell are you two doing here!"

"Megan sent us," Anthony said. He rubbed my thigh reassuringly. "We had to bring you back. This whole thing with the Secret Service hiding you away in the middle of bum-fuck Ohio? It's all a bullshit excuse by POTUS to make you seem weak. Hide you away after your announcement like a coward."

"You didn't have to wear masks!"

Ethan scoffed, his hands tightening on the steering wheel as we flew down the dirt road. "We knew Captain Serious-Face wouldn't disobey orders and let you leave. So we took things into our own hands. And we had to keep our identities secret since it's sorta, kinda, maybe illegal to restrain a Secret Service Agent with duct tape."

"Restrain him?" I asked. "You shot him!"

"Only with a bean bag shotgun," Anthony clarified.

"Hell of a shot from that range," Ethan said.

Anthony grinned. "I know, right?"

"He was in pain! You might have broken one of his bones!"

Anthony rolled his eyes. "I knocked the wind out of him. It'll leave a huge welt, but he'll be fine."

My eyes widened. "Boomer! What did you do to Boomer?"

"Who? The dog?" Ethan asked. "He was a sweetie. Lured him with a juicy steak stuffed with sedatives in it, Scooby Doo style. He's taking a nap in the woods."

"I put a blanket over him," Anthony added. "We're not monsters."

I began to relax. I *had* wanted a way out of the cabin. This wasn't how I would have gone about it, but I was finally going back to Washington. *And I had just gotten used to the simple life.*

"Relax, sugar," Anthony insisted. His hand remained on my thigh, a warm and comforting presence. "You're safe with us now."

"How did you find me?"

"You can thank your campaign manager for that," Ethan said with a chuckle. "She saw a remote login to your email address. Traced that IP address to a cell phone hotspot, then called in some favors to track it to a cell tower down here. From there she figured out that Agent Santos had a family cabin in range of the tower."

"It was impressive," Anthony said. "Real detective shit."

"Megan is nothing if not persistent," I muttered. "Before working for me, she was fired from another campaign for doing something shady like that."

"Elizabeth," Ethan said. "You didn't *want* to be hidden away down here, right?"

"Of course not," I said. "Why would you suggest that?"

He shrugged his shoulders. "I thought you'd be happier to be rescued by us."

"No, I *am* happy," I insisted, reaching up to squeeze his shoulder. "I'm just in shock. And still a little confused. How did the two of you pair up to look for me?"

Anthony barked a laugh. "Your bodyguard tackled me in the crowd in Columbus. Thought I was a threat, even though I was working with the Columbus PD to search for threats in the crowd. Can you believe he thought my walkie-talkie was a gun?"

"My view was obscured!" Ethan protested. "Plus, you *were* the guy tailing us on the motorcycle. I was right to be suspicious."

"Anyway, so he tackles me. Then the *real* gunshots went off," Anthony continued. "Everything was chaos, people screaming and running for their lives. Before we knew what was happening, Agent Santos had you whisked away to a hospital. By the time Megan and us got there, you were gone again. To an undisclosed location. They wouldn't tell us anything."

"We met up with Ms. Hanram after that since we didn't know what else to do," Ethan said. His eyes met mine in the rear-view mirror, and he cleared his throat awkwardly. "That's when Anthony told us."

"Told you what?"

"That he was your boyfriend."

33

Elizabeth

Boyfriend.

He'd told them that he was my boyfriend.

"I... um... what?" I managed to say.

"I couldn't stand around doing nothing, and I couldn't try to find you on my own," Anthony explained. His hand was still on my thigh. "I know you wanted to keep *us* a secret, but I had to come clean with them. It was the only way to convince them to let me help find you."

Ethan stared at me in the mirror. Waiting to see what I would say about this.

Boyfriend. Oh lord.

I wanted to explain that of course he wasn't my boyfriend. That he was just a Capitol Policeman I'd hooked up with because I was lonely on my birthday. But I also didn't want to upset Anthony by minimizing our relationship. If you could even call it that.

And I *really* didn't want to have this conversation right now.

I should have stuck with anonymous escorts in hotel rooms.

"Where is Megan?" I asked.

"Back in Washington," Anthony said. "She's been working 20 hour days doing damage control for your disappearance. Canceling all the interviews and appearances she'd lined up, and scheduling new ones for when you hopefully reappear. That woman is a force of nature."

"She's the best," I said. "What's the plan? Fly out of Columbus?"

"Megan insisted we drive back," Ethan said. Was his voice colder now? More detached? "Tomorrow is President's Day. A number of senators are giving speeches in front of the Washington Monument. Megan wants you to crash the event, make a speech. Generate a bunch of buzz."

"Of course she does," I said, shaking my head.

"We'll stop for the night in Virginia and make the final leg of the trip in the morning. Secrecy will get us the biggest media boost when you *do* appear, so we're laying low tonight."

Anthony handed me a piece of paper. "Here's the speech she wrote for you. She wants you to memorize it before tomorrow morning." From his tone, he thought that would be impossible.

"Not a problem. It's only three paragraphs," I said. Anthony's jaw dropped so I added, "Being a politician means being good at memorizing speeches. Normally I have only a few minutes to prepare. Having an entire car ride back to Washington is luxury."

Anthony laughed, but Ethan remained silent behind the wheel.

*

We drove through southern Ohio, old mining towns similar to where I had grown up. The sun had set by the time we crossed into West Virginia and climbed up and down the winding roads that traversed the Appalachian Mountains. We stopped only to fill up on gas and buy greasy fast food for dinner. After eating some form of venison for 10 straight meals my burger and fries tasted *fantastic*.

We passed into Virginia and drove up I-81, eventually reaching Harrisonburg at 9:30 at night. Ethan stopped at a small motel on the northern edge of town, which was deserted except for a single car in the back of the parking lot. If not for the light on in the small lobby I would have assumed it was closed.

"James Madison University is in Harrisonburg," Anthony said absently while we walked to our rooms. "You think they'll ever name a school after you?" Elizabeth O'Hare College."

"I have to win first," I said. "But I do like the sound of that."

"I guess only the really old presidents get colleges named after them," Anthony said. "I've never heard of a Carter or Bush university."

"She's not even running for president," Ethan snapped. "She wants a VP spot."

"What? Why?" Anthony stared at me. "You can win the whole thing. You're 35 now."

Ethan rolled his eyes.

"We'll see," was all I said.

I had a room to myself, while the boys were sharing another. "We need to be on the road by 5:00am at the latest," Ethan said. "We'll be right next door if you need anything. Just scream. We have the spare key to your room just in case."

He went inside his room without another word. Anthony gave me a wink before following.

I stepped into my room and let the door swing shut behind me. The room was clean and smelled fresh. Couldn't ask for more than that.

I dropped my suitcase into the lone chair by the door and sat on the edge of the bed. I had remained in shock for most of the drive here, but now I was finally beginning to process everything. The campaign trail would be a lot of this: long days and short nights in hotel rooms before waking up early and starting all over again. It was exhausting to think about.

But after my few days of relaxation with Luca, I was almost ready for the grind. Deep down I was itching for the opportunity to do what I did best: campaign. Convincing people to vote for me, that I would do the best job representing their interests. It was what I was born to do.

Three days in a cabin couldn't change who I was.

The cabin. I felt a pang of regret for Luca. I hoped he wouldn't get in too much trouble for allowing me to be taken. More than that, I hoped he wasn't upset at me. I *did* warn him that I would have to make an escape eventually. I'd been mostly joking at the time.

Maybe I could look up his number and call him. Apologize for what happened. Mostly I felt guilty for abandoning him so quickly without so much as a goodbye, even though it wasn't my fault that I'd been hauled away kicking and screaming.

I showered and changed into the pajamas from my suitcase. As soon as I had my top on, someone knocked on my door. I checked the peep hole before opening it. Ethan shouldered his way into my room before I could say hello. The door clicked closed behind him.

"Boyfriend?" he demanded.

"I'm glad you're here, because I wanted to talk about that..."

"He's your *boyfriend?*" Ethan repeated. "Seriously?"

I patted the air to calm him down. "That's not what Anthony is."

"Then what is he, Elizabeth?" Pain was in Ethan's green eyes. And even a hint of tears. He was hurt. That realization sent guilt searing through my throat.

I sat him down and explained everything. How we'd hooked up on my birthday after he was assigned to watch my apartment, but that it was short-lived. I held Ethan's hand and tried to pour as much regret as I could through his touch.

"I'm sorry I didn't tell you," I said. "I didn't think I really needed to. I didn't realize how much Anthony liked me until he followed us to Ohio. I especially didn't want to make you jealous."

Ethan sighed. "Jealous? I'm relieved."

"Really?"

"I was afraid he was more than that. It made me think I was just a side-fling for you compared to your serious boyfriend."

I laughed bitterly. "I'm not allowed to have a steady boyfriend. Especially during the campaign. You're seriously not jealous? It's okay if you are."

His handsome face turned toward me. "I was already kind of used to the idea when you were just a client of mine in a hotel room. I assumed you had a husband or something. The fact that you're actually single, and Anthony is just a boy toy on the side is a huge relief." He shook his head. "My biggest fear..."

"What?" I asked gently.

"My biggest fear was that I was only a physical release for you. That you didn't like anything else about me."

I caressed his cheek. "Oh, Ethan. That may be how it started, but I like a lot of things about you. I'm scared by how much I like you."

"Good," he said. "Because Anthony and I are sort of friends now."

"Hah! Seriously?"

"Anthony is a good guy. He cares about you the same way I care about you. He's driven to protect you, which I can relate to. We've sort of bonded in the last few days while tracking you down."

"Does he know?" I asked. "About you and I?"

"No. I'm kind of worried about what he'll say when he finds out."

A knock came on the door, and then Anthony used the spare key to unlock it and come inside. "Dude, I thought you went to get ice."

"Got sidetracked on the way. Sit down. We all need to talk."

Anthony froze and looked at both of us before closing the door and joining us. My room had two double beds, and the two of them sat on one while I sat on the other, facing them.

"Anthony," I said gently, "I have to tell you something."

"You've been sleeping with Ethan?"

Ethan and I both flinched. "How'd you know?"

Anthony grinned sheepishly, and elbowed Ethan in the ribs. "I've been with this dude nonstop for the last 48 hours. I can tell he's got a big old crush on you. And he had the same drive to find you that I had. So yeah, I could tell. You've got a thing for the people protecting you, huh?"

"No..." I began, but then thought of Luca in the cabin. All the fun we'd had. Tying me to the bed with chains and licking every inch of my body...

Shoot. Maybe I *did* have a thing for the people protecting me.

"Yeah, Ethan and I have a history. Which we are *not* going to go into in great detail right now," I said, giving Ethan a sharp look. "The bottom line is I like both of you. We've had some great times together. But I really must reiterate: my campaign for the presidency is beginning *now*. As much as I would love to keep things going with both of you, I just can't risk the scrutiny to my campaign."

"I understand," Ethan said. Anthony nodded, but looked unhappy.

"It's better for both of you as well," I added. "If anyone found out you were romantically involved with a presidential candidate, you'd have reporters and paparazzi all over you 24/7. Your lives would be *miserable*. We wouldn't be able to enjoy our time together."

"I know," Anthony grumbled. He looked at me with those deep, dark eyes. "I hate it, but I *get* it. I'll do whatever you need me to do for the rest of your campaign. Even if that means quietly going away."

Ethan spun his head around. "Seriously?"

"Of course," Anthony said.

"Why are you surprised?" I asked.

My jaw dropped as Ethan told me the reason why.

34

Anthony

Alright, so I made a mistake.

I'd burned some vacation time to take my little road trip to Ohio. My boss grumbled but gave in, especially since I'd had to discharge my weapon just a week prior when Elizabeth was first attacked. They tried to give cops who did that a long leash. Undue stress after a traumatic event was never good for anyone.

Following Elizabeth to Columbus felt *right*. Like I was going where I was needed. Helping keep the senator safe while she gave her speech on the steps of the Ohio Statehouse. It was more exciting, more fulfilling, than just giving out speeding tickets on the beltway.

So was working with Ethan to track her down

since the Secret Service essentially kidnapped her. Following digital breadcrumbs with the help of Megan. Planning Elizabeth's rescue. Breaking a few federal laws and risking everything to get the senator back in our car and on her way back to Washington where she belonged.

So, when my boss finally called yesterday and demanded to know where I was? I told him to shove it, because I quit.

I wasn't going back to escorting motorcades and checking meters after this.

Elizabeth got a funny look on her face. "Why are you surprised?"

Ethan jerked his thumb toward me. "This guy quit his job at the USCP. For you."

"What!"

"Not just for you," I quickly said. I gave Ethan a look: *dude*. "I was sick of the Capitol Police. They were always giving me the shit duties. Said I had too much of an attitude."

"Shit duties like watching a senator's house?" Elizabeth said with her wide, gorgeous smile. Fuck. Giving up everything had been worth it just to see that smile again. I'd throw myself in front of a semi if I thought it would make her happy.

"That's the kind of job I *do* want," I said. "I want to work for you. I want to be your bodyguard."

She stared at me, waiting to see if I was making

a joke. "You want to take Ethan's place?"

"We can both be bodyguards," I insisted. "One sure isn't good enough to keep you safe."

"I could definitely use an extra man," Ethan admitted. "Especially after this last attack. The more eyes, the better."

"I just told you I can't have any temptation on the campaign trail," Elizabeth said. "And you think becoming my bodyguard will somehow make that *easier* for you?"

It was a question I'd been asking myself since I quit my job: whether or not I could handle being around Elizabeth so much without touching her.

I knew the answer: *no*. An emphatic *no*.

It would drive me crazy. Even now, with the way Elizabeth leaned forward on the bed and showed off a little bit of cleavage, the urge to rip her clothes off and *take her* was overpowering. There was no way I could resist that temptation for the entirety of the campaign.

"Yes," I said. It was an easy lie. I would say anything to stay by her side for the foreseeable future. "I will do whatever I can to protect you, even if that means being completely platonic. Whatever is best for you. And your campaign."

"Do you really mean that?" she asked softly. Her eyes were wide and waiting. She *wanted* to believe it, even if she knew it was a lie.

"With all my heart," I said.

She looked at Ethan. "I'll do my best," he said.

Elizabeth closed her eyes and smiled. "I'm happy to hear that."

She closed the distance between us, grabbed my face with both hands, and kissed me. Her tongue danced in my mouth as I fell backwards on the bed, her thighs straddling me.

She had a way of turning off my brain, erasing the entire world so that all I could think about was her. Until Ethan cleared his throat, reminding us that he was on the bed next to us.

Elizabeth panted as she sat up. Her face was flushed and her nipples were hard against her pajamas. The same silk pajamas she'd been wearing the first night I was with her, on her birthday.

"I want you," she told me. Then she slid over to Ethan. "I want both of you."

I watched as she straddled him the way she'd straddled me, then French kissed Ethan so hard it knocked him onto his back. I took a moment to examine my feelings. I was watching Elizabeth, the woman I was obsessed with, kiss another man. A guy I'd befriended in the past few days, bonding over our desire to find the senator.

Strange as it was, I didn't feel jealous.

In fact, it kind of turned me on. Awakening something new inside.

I watched hungrily as she ground against his crotch, her ass plump and tight in her pajama bottoms. I'd never had a threesome before. I'd fantasized about them like any hot-blooded man, but it always involved two women rather than two men.

I ran my hand over Elizabeth's back, feeling the silk pressing against her smooth skin while she dry-humped my new friend. I took hold of her shirt and pulled it over her head, and she raised her arms to let me, exposing her full breasts. Ethan rose and took one of them in his mouth, drawing a sigh from Elizabeth's plump lips.

I kissed her bare back and ran my hands over her, pausing at the stitching along her side. The bullet wound. It was red but not swollen, and the lines of black stitching looked like railroad tracks.

My lips slid down to press against the wound, a wordless way of letting her know we were going to protect her. She flinched at the touch, then sighed some more.

Ethan and I met eyes. A silent understanding passed between us. We would do whatever it took to protect Elizabeth from danger, even if it meant giving up our lives. And we would enjoy her tonight, even if it was the last time.

Especially if it was the last time.

She laid flat on Ethan's body and I pulled her pajama bottoms off, exposing pink cotton panties, the middle wet with her juices. I pulled those off even slower, letting my fingertips drag on her skin as I did. She kissed Ethan and shivered.

"Fuck me," she said, and I didn't know if she was talking to me or Ethan. "I need you to fuck me."

Ethan and I smiled as one and set to obliging the senator.

35

Elizabeth

The only thing hotter than two gorgeous men were two gorgeous men who were completely devoted to protecting me. I could see it in their eyes and expressions. They would die for me.

I've never wanted a threesome so badly in my life.

Anthony responded to my command by saying, "I want to fuck you."

"Don't keep her waiting," Ethan said, cupping the side of my face and pulling me back down into a kiss.

I sighed into Ethan's mouth while Anthony removed his clothes, the belt buckle clinking as his pants fell to the floor. Then he stepped up to me, his thighs against my thighs. The head of his cock rubbed up against my clit, then back and into my waiting lips.

"She likes it hard," Ethan said. "Give it to her."

As if he'd been waiting for permission, Anthony's cock sank into me. The wonderful pressure of manhood deep inside my lady parts, expanding my inner walls on all sides. I bit down on Ethan's lip by accident, but not enough to draw blood. His grin widened.

"Yeah. She likes that alright."

"Oh, I *do*..."

Anthony grabbed hold of my waist and pumped me from behind while Ethan French kissed me some. Four hands gripped me and stroked me and caressed me, twice as much love as I'd ever had before.

"My turn," Ethan said after maybe 20 seconds.

He wriggled underneath me to undo his pants, then kicked them off with his foot. Ethan reached between us and guided himself up and in. I pushed my hips down onto him, taking him in one quick stroke.

"There it is," Ethan half-said, half-moaned. "What I've been thinking about for the last week."

Ethan wasn't as long as Anthony, but he was wider, which felt just as good but in a different way. The difference in their hardware was exciting when experienced only seconds apart.

I pressed my hand into his rugged chest and rode him like a cowgirl. His blond surfer hair fell across his face as he rolled his head in ecstasy, eyes locked onto mine.

"My turn again," Anthony said possessively. I lifted myself off Ethan long enough for his cock to slip out and slide against my belly, and without hesitation Anthony shoved his prick back inside me and resumed right where he'd left off.

"Oh yeah," Ethan said. His dick slid up and down my belly, dry-humping me while Anthony *really* fucked me. "How's she feel, man?"

"Like heaven," Anthony said, fingers digging into my hips. "Like I'm gonna come soon."

"That's why we're alternating," Ethan said smoothly. "So we last longer. So she gets as much of us as she can."

"I want *all* of you," I said, letting my head hang down over Ethan while Anthony pumped me from behind. "Don't stop!"

Anthony groaned with ecstasy as he sped up, his shaft sliding deeper and deeper inside. "I have to..."

He pulled out with a sigh, leaving me hollow. But Ethan was quick to pick up the slack, using his thighs to guide himself down and then up inside of me. I gasped as he filled me completely again, and this time he held me down while *he* pumped his hips up into me.

I glanced over my shoulder and saw Anthony stroking himself while watching. "How's the view back there?" I said in a lusty voice.

"The view is great. Fucking hell, you have a nice ass."

"Then take it," the words slipped out of my mouth before I could stop them, but once they were out I knew it was what I'd wanted. I hadn't done anal with a guy in a *long* time, but tonight was the right night. "Take my ass, Anthony."

His eyes widened with hunger.

"You heard her. Fuck her in the ass." Ethan licked his middle finger like a lollipop and then guided it around, using the saliva to rub against my tight, forbidden hole. "I'll warm her up for ya."

"Oh!" I moaned deeply as the tip of his finger pressed into my back door. It slid in easily thanks to the saliva, a full inch, then two. Ethan held his finger inside my ass while continuing to fuck me from underneath, slowly and steadily.

"Fucking hell, that's hot," Anthony said.

"Then take it," I repeated. "Take my ass. I'm ready."

I didn't *really* know if I was ready. But I was excited to find out.

Then, he slid both his finger and his dick out

of me. My lips quivered with excitement as Anthony approached, a ravenous look on his beautiful face. But he didn't stick it in my ass: he stuck it back in my pussy, two slow strokes.

Getting himself wet, I realized as he pulled out. He pressed the head against my forbidden ring. I relaxed, and slowly it pressed deeper. Without warning my asshole engulfed the entire tip.

Anthony groaned at the same time that I sighed.

"Your ass is so tight!" he said. "Goddamn."

Ethan reached around and gave my ass cheek a hard slap. "She always looked like she had a tight ass."

I moaned as Anthony began trying to push deeper. He didn't really go anywhere; all it did was push me forward on Ethan's chest. But slowly, inch by inch, my ass devoured more of his cock. He stayed rock hard inside of me despite the lack of direct stimulation.

Ethan leaned up and took one of my nipples in his mouth again, gently sucking and swirling his tongue around and around. That, paired with the tip of Anthony's prick shoved in my ass, gave me an intense shudder. I looked back at him. The tension in his neck made his tattoos writhe and dance while he focused on my nether region.

I closed my eyes and rocked back and forth from their joined efforts.

And then Ethan said, "Time to switch it up."

He gestured to Anthony, something I couldn't

see. Then Anthony wrapped his arms around my chest and pulled me off my other bodyguard until my back was stuck to his chest. All the while my tight ring clutched the tip of his penis like it never wanted to let go. Anthony sat on the edge, then lay back flat, pulling me with him so that I was laying with my back on his chest. Ethan hopped up and stood in between my legs, then rubbed my wet slit up and down.

"Let's get those juices moving," he said, rubbing harder and harder. The weight of my hips and gravity pushed my pelvis lower on Anthony's steel rod, and he moaned into my ear behind me.

Ethan, a tall god of tan muscle, spread my legs and then sank his cock into my waiting sex. The sound I made was surprise and excitement and pleasure as I felt their dual members pressing inside me, sandwiching my inner wall.

"There we go," Ethan crooned in his deep voice.

His body rolled up and down like ocean waves as he steadily fucked me. It made me so wet that my juices slid down and began coating Anthony's firm cock beneath me, lubing it up so that I continued sliding further down him, impaling myself deeper and deeper.

"Now I'm the one who's gonna come," Ethan sneered. "*Fuck*, you're even tighter with Anthony in your ass."

Underneath me, Anthony wrapped two arms around and squeezed my breasts. "I'll say she is."

Watching Ethan's chiseled body work between my legs was like watching erotic porn. No man had a right to look so gorgeous, let alone a man who was presently filling me with every inch of his manhood! The stimulation from him inside my pussy and Anthony deeper and deeper inside my ass was almost more than I could handle. I touched myself, which made Ethan's smile deepen.

"There you go," he said, sweat now glistening on his muscles. "Come for us, Senator O'Hare."

Hearing my title was a lightning bolt of ecstasy that scoured my bones. I rubbed a fire into my clit and my cries grew louder and louder.

Anthony moved underneath me, his cock sliding up and down in my ass now with frictionless ease. Whether intentional or not, my two bodyguards' strokes soon coordinated, so that they were both pulling back at the same time and thrusting into me simultaneously.

"Such a tight ass," Anthony groaned, a warning in his voice. "I'm gonna fill it... with... my... *come...*"

The last word turned into a roar as he pumped my ass with his seed. His spasms threw me over the edge and I opened my mouth, exhaling all my breath as my climax became so intense that I couldn't breathe.

Ethan's roars of orgasm were loudest of all, and his eyes never left me as he filled my pussy with his warm seed.

36

Elizabeth

We were up and on the road no later than 5:00am, just as Ethan had demanded. It was going to be a long day and we still had close to two hours to go before we reached the city. I spent most of the time chugging bad hotel coffee we'd brought with us in small paper cups and reviewing my speech again. By the time we stopped in Reston for breakfast burritos I was ready.

"I just thought of something," I said from the back seat after we'd all eaten.

"Was it how you love getting double-penetrated by two hot guys?" Ethan asked from behind the wheel, a smile on his lips. "Because I've thought about nothing *but* that since last night."

"Emphasis on the *butt*," Anthony added with an immature laugh.

"I've been thinking about that too," I said, unable to hide my own private smile. "But just now I realized: what happens if the Secret Service figures out it was you who kidnapped—I mean *rescued*—me?"

"Good question," Ethan said.

Anthony rubbed his neck tattoos. "Maybe we can act like we didn't *know* it was the Secret Service. Pretend like we thought you were kidnapped by one of the assassins." He looked at Ethan. "That's plausible, right?"

"Except for the fact that I've worked with Agent Santos before," he said. "I can't pretend that I didn't recognize him."

"Oh. Right."

"We'll worry about all that later," Ethan said with a shrug. "All that matters now is Elizabeth is safe."

I reached up and put a hand on each of their shoulders. "I feel safe."

"The media is going to go nuts when you reappear," Anthony said. He was looking at his phone. "Social media is calling this *Day Five* of O'Hare-Watch."

I took the phone from him and read through the comments. Momentum hadn't died down in the days since my announcement slash shooting. If anything, it had risen to an almost explosive level. Everyone wanted to know where Candidate O'Hare was. If she was really okay after the shooting. What she had to say about it.

Megan is probably going nuts waiting for me to return.

Washington had a variety of events happening for President's Day. Most of them were later in the day, but the signs were evident as we drove along the National Mall: stages being erected, porta-potties dropped off for a President's Day 5k Run, and a handful of other charity-related events.

"Are we not going to my apartment?" I asked.

"People are probably watching it," Ethan said. "The last thing we want is the Secret Service whisking you away again before you can make your grand appearance. We're meeting Megan in your Capitol office."

"And that *won't* be watched?" I asked.

"Not with Megan there. She's been shouting at anyone who dares get close enough to disrupt her work. We think we can get you inside without raising too much of a fuss."

We drove down into the Capitol garage and showed our credentials at the gate. The security guard visibly mouthed my name when he read it off the license, then stared for a long time at me in the back seat. I smiled and waved back.

It was easier once we were parked and inside the building. I was still wearing the cotton beanie Luca had given me for our hike, and with most of my hair covered nobody recognized me in the hall. I stepped into my office to find Megan pacing back and forth while on the phone. Her face lit up when she saw me.

"I'll call you back," she said and hung up the phone, then wrapped me in a tight hug. "Oh, Elizabeth. It's so good to see your face! A face which needs makeup. No offense."

I smiled at my long-time campaign manager. "Always focused on the job."

"That's why you hired me."

She ushered me into the chair and called in a makeup and hair stylist, a young woman who didn't seem impressed to be working on the missing Senator O'Hare. She immediately began toying with my hair and setting to work with her makeup bag.

"You two can wait outside," Megan said, shoving my bodyguards out the door and closing it behind them. When she turned back to me, tears were in her almond eyes. "I can't forgive myself for what happened at the Ohio Statehouse. Getting shot... If I had known that would happen I never would have made you announce that day! You have to believe me, Elizabeth..."

I took her hand in mine and squeezed it. I was touched by how emotional she was getting. Maybe I hadn't processed the shooting as much as I needed to.

"It's not your fault," I said. "There's no point in trying to take any blame for it."

She wiped her eyes and shook her head. "I know. It's just..." She waved a hand. "I'm glad to see Ethan and your... *friend* were able to rescue you without issue."

Oh, crap. Anthony had told her he was my boyfriend. Megan knew that I had slept with him. And right before I announced my candidacy, no less. I steeled myself for her ridicule. A long lecture about how reckless it was to sleep with *anyone* on a whim, let alone the USCP officer assigned to watch my apartment. I deserved whatever shouting she would do.

But she only smiled. "You've got good taste, I must admit. He has delicious tattoos. Mmm!"

I cocked my head. "Are... Are you okay, Megan?"

She sipped from a mug of coffee, then winced. "Aside from a lack of sleep? I'm fine." She gestured at the makeup girl. "What are you waiting for? Get started. We have a speech to crash in less than an hour!"

The girl made a distasteful noise while she began adding product to my hair.

Megan disappeared to make several more calls, then returned when my hair was drying. "We have so much to catch up on, Elizabeth, but for now I'll give you the crash course. Several congressmen and congresswomen are giving speeches in front of the Washington Monument this morning. Two of them are candidates you'll be up against in the primary... Including Senator Pollock."

"Oh?" I asked.

"Mmm hmm. I've been spending a lot of our campaign funds on polling data over the last few days, and you know what the tea leaves say? You're neck-and-neck with Pollock. Scoring higher on the likability index, too."

"That's fantastic!"

"That's not even the good news." She leaned in and smiled. "Pollock's campaign manager reached out to me last night. A cocky asshole named Trevor, but that's beside the point. Pollock's campaign is interested in you. They want to cooperate with our campaign. You'll back each other up during the primary debates. And then, when it's all done, Pollock will choose *you* to be his running mate!"

My heart almost stopped beating. "You're joking."

She frowned at me. "Sweetie, you know I never joke. We've done it. There's going to be a Pollock-O'Hare ticket!"

I bounced up and down in my chair, which frustrated the makeup girl, but I was too giddy to care. *We'd done it.* The campaign hadn't even been official for a week and we had already accomplished the goal.

"It's all unofficial of course, but I'm going to hammer *Trevor* to get it in writing. The last thing I want is for you to go soft on Pollock in the debates and then they pull the rug out from under us and tap some spineless yes-man like Hollenbach for their ticket. But first, you need to make your grand reappearance!" She snapped her fingers at the makeup girl. "Why have you stopped? We're on a tight schedule!"

A knock came on the door. Ethan poked his head in. "Uhh, Senator O'Hare? We have a problem."

"No problems," Megan said. "We cannot have any problems at this stage of the plan. Take your problems elsewhere, you handsome man."

But Ethan moved out of the way, and someone else replaced him.

The last person I expected to see walked into the room.

37

Elizabeth

Agent Luca Santos had an apologetic smile on his face. "Am I interrupting anything, Senator O'Hare?"

Ahh, crap. I knew this confrontation was inevitable, but I had hoped it wouldn't happen for a few more days. Luca was back to wearing his suit and tie, which was almost a strange sight after seeing him dressed more like a mountain man at the cabin.

I leaned back in my chair and sighed. "I warned you I would eventually make my escape."

"I guess it's on me for not taking you more seriously." He twisted. "My back is still sore from that bean bag shotgun. I'm not used to sleeping on my side."

Megan let out an exasperated noise. "Agent Santos, you're the last person we need in our face right now. You're not going to ruin this for us, are you?"

A dark look passed over his face as he rounded on my campaign manager. "You hired those two goons outside to kidnap Elizabeth and bring her back to Washington."

She wasn't fazed by his intimidating posture. She stepped up and glared right back at him. "Agent Santos, I would do anything for this woman's campaign. *Anything*. Do not get in our way."

"I wasn't kidnapped by Ethan and Anthony," I said. "If anything, what the Secret Service did was kidnapping."

Anger flared up on Luca's face. "Is that all you have to say about the last three days? That I held you against your will, and you're glad to be back?"

I rose from my chair, ignoring the makeup girl's annoyed scoff. "Of course not. I enjoyed our time together at the cabin. But you know I couldn't stay forever."

I was afraid the fire wouldn't leave his eyes. That he would never forgive me, or that it would take so long that it might as well have been forever. Slowly, his face softened.

"I know, Elizabeth."

Megan made an annoyed noise and pointed her

finger back and forth between us. "We'll discuss what's going on *here* later. Agent Santos, are you going to ruin all of this or not? Because if you are, I would like to request that you wait an hour so we can at least make our speech first."

"I should take you back right this instant," he said. "My superiors don't know you have escaped yet. They think you're still hidden away in the middle of nowhere. There's still time to get you back before they figure it out." Then he shook his head. "But I don't care about any of that. I would be doing a disservice to the world keeping you hidden away when you're in such high demand. Ships in harbors, and all that."

"You don't care that you'll get in trouble?" I asked. "The moment I make that speech..."

"I'm done caring," he said. "They'll find a way to be unhappy with me regardless of what happens. So we might as well do what's best for *you*. Elizabeth, I want to stay by your side. Not just while you have a Secret Service detail, but throughout the campaign. I'll be your private bodyguard. I'll keep you safe."

"Luca..." I didn't know what to say. The insistence in his eyes, the warmth and confidence in his voice, made my throat constrict.

"Our campaign would gladly hire you," Megan said. "Three bodyguards is better than two, and after all the donations we've received this week we can easily afford it."

"Two?" Luca asked. "Wait. Don't tell me you

hired that tatted up punk outside."

"That's the USCP officer Ethan tackled at the Columbus event," I said. "He was the cop on duty when I was attacked outside my apartment. The one who shot my attacker. He's proven that he's trustworthy."

He squinted at me. Studying me. Had I given away too much talking about Anthony? Luca was perceptive—maybe he could tell I had feelings for my other bodyguard.

The makeup girl coughed conspicuously.

"You need to get out of our hair so Elizabeth can finish *her* hair. Go on, shoo. Outside with the other chiseled hunks who want to throw down their lives for our dear senator. Goodbye." She closed the door and rested her back against it. "You have a type, Elizabeth."

"It's not what you—"

"We'll talk about it later," she said. A grin tugged on one side of her mouth. "Over a bottle of wine. I want to hear *all* the juicy details."

We left my office with 20 minutes to go before the speech. Out in the hallway my three bodyguards were milling around like husbands at a cookout.

"You look stunning, senator," Ethan said.

Anthony winked at me and said, "Mmm hmm. You're gonna knock 'em dead."

"You've got a couple of suck-ups out here," Luca

told me.

"Unlike *you,* we work directly for Senator O'Hare's campaign," Anthony said. "We've got to keep the boss happy, whether via compliments or anything else."

I flashed Anthony a look of surprise. Luca held out his palm.

"Relax. We all had a long talk out here." He looked at Anthony, then Ethan. "We're all on the same page about you, Senator O'Hare."

"Oh," I said. Damnit, why did their combined stares make me blush? "Good. Now you can focus on actually keeping me safe."

We walked out to the deck of the Capitol Building, overlooking the National Mall. The tall Washington Monument rose above the park, pale white against the clear blue sky. That's where the speeches were occurring. I would have to march almost a mile to get there.

Good thing I was wearing flats.

"I don't like how much open space there is," Luca said, gazing around from behind his black sunglasses. He was right: there were dozens of rooftops and open windows on either side of the mall where a shooter would have a clear shot. I felt a tingle of fear as I remembered how my last public appearance had gone.

"Gonna have to agree with the Super Special Agent," Anthony said. "It'll be awfully tough to protect you all the way to the monument. Unless we practically sandwich Elizabeth between our bodies."

He gave me a secret smile at that last part. Memories of last night ran through my head before I fought them down.

Not now, Elizabeth. Focus!

Still, I gave Anthony a knowing smile in return.

"Nobody knows you're here," Megan said dismissively. "You'll be fine."

Luca shook his head. "We don't know that for sure. If the assassin has been watching you, Megan, then they could know Elizabeth is here. They could be watching us right now."

"I think it's Elizabeth's call," Ethan said. "It's her campaign." Anthony nodded in agreement.

Megan put a hand on my shoulder. "Elizabeth. I want you to trust me. You are 100% safe right now. Nothing is going to happen to you."

Something in her words, her look, and her touch convinced me. Having her with me again filled me with confidence. "Then let's go crash these speeches."

We walked down the steps to the National Mall, and then my three bodyguards took up a formation around me. Anthony a few steps to my left, Ethan to the right, and Luca walking behind with Megan. Anthony and Ethan dropped back a step so that I was leading the way. They were following me, not escorting me.

The National Mall was filled with its usual crowd of tourists and people who were there for the various President's Day events. Lots of families out enjoying the surprisingly warm morning, taking photos of the Capitol Building and the Washington Monument. My little parade had made it about 100 yards before I heard someone from a tour group say, "Isn't that the missing senator?"

After that, the flood gates of comments opened.

"That's O'Hare!"

"Elizabeth O'Hare! She's alive!"

"I told you it wasn't all some conspiracy to cover up her death..."

"Senator O'Hare! Can I get a photo!"

Like a school of sharks attacking chum, the people crowded around. My bodyguards looked uncomfortable at so many people getting close, but I couldn't allow myself to be afraid. If a politician couldn't mingle with her potential constituents, she didn't deserve to be a politician.

I took selfies with teenagers and adults alike, and signed dozens of autographs. But I never slowed my stride. Onward we marched toward the Washington Monument with a growing number of people following behind, like a comet with a long tail. Dozens of runners from the President's Day 5k Run pulled away from their route to join our group. Soon I was surrounded on all sides, in front and behind, by people of every age and background. A steel welder from Cincinnati said that he'd voted for me in the senate election, and couldn't wait to vote for me in the presidential primary. A kindergarten teacher from Baltimore asked if I was going to expand classroom supply tax write-offs, to which I told her that we were *already* working on a bill to that end in the senate, even before I ran for president.

Soon the crowd noise was a constant din all around me. Cheers and shouts and even a short-lived "Oh-Hare! Oh-Hare!" chant. By the time I reached the Washington Monument I had an entire army at my back.

This was what I was born to do. This was who I *was*.

The stage was about 30 feet wide with steps on the side, a podium in the center, and a red, white, and blue backdrop of the American flag. The crowd wasn't very large, and was mostly made up of the press pool in the back. All the press there to hear Senator Pollock speak.

His speech drifted across the space with the aid of speakers. He paused and looked out at our arriving crowd and said, "It looks like someone is here to protest my stance on equal pay."

The press pool turned and began snapping photos. I don't know when they realized it was me at the center of the crowd, but suddenly everyone was jostling to get close for photographs and microphone interviews.

The crowd at my back merged with the crowd for the speech, and then my bodyguards cleared a path over to the side of the stage.

Megan leaned in close so I could hear her. "You ready?"

"I am."

"The pressure is off. You've got the VP slot locked in with Pollock." She gripped me by the shoulders. "I promised I would get you to this point, no matter what it took. Well, here we are. We did it, Elizabeth. Think of this as a victory speech."

Pollock left the stage and came down the stairs. Though he was pushing 60, he looked sharp in a blue suit and a red tie. "Senator O'Hare? You're here!" His tan face was surprised, even shocked.

And as I looked into his eyes, I was struck with a flash of insight.

I knew who had been trying to kill me.

38

Elizabeth

"Senator Pollock," I said, shaking his hand. "It's great to see you, but if you'll excuse me for a moment..."

I turned away from the stage.

"Where are you going?" Megan asked.

"I need to talk to you."

"We can talk later. The stage is set for you to—"

"*Now*," I hissed.

She shut up and followed me away from the crowd. "What's wrong?" Luca asked on the other side of her.

"Nothing," I said. "Just give us some space real quick."

"You sure?" Anthony asked over my left shoulder.

"Yep. But stay close."

Megan had a curious look on her face as I stopped behind a tree to give us a little privacy. My three bodyguards stayed a respectable distance away, but glanced over every few seconds. They were wondering what all this was about.

I looked at my campaign manager. Dressed in jeans and a comfortable blouse underneath her jacket, with her hair pulled back in an easy ponytail. She always did choose functionality over form for herself. Entirely focused on the goal of getting me elected rather than her own looks.

"Elizabeth," she said impatiently. "What's going on?"

"I don't know how I didn't see it before," I said. "You promised you would get me here. No matter what it cost. No matter what you had to do. You've said that often over the past few campaigns. Almost like a mantra."

She hesitated before saying, "Of course."

"The night before I was attacked outside my apartment, you reminded me to go jogging. Insisted on it."

"I wanted you sharp the next day," she said.

"For the Finance Committee hearings. You know you're always best when you make time for your morning jog."

"But I *always* get my jog in," I said. "There's no point in reminding me. Unless you wanted to *really* make sure I did it that specific morning. Because you knew someone was going to be waiting."

"Elizabeth..."

"Then at the Ohio Statehouse, during my candidacy announcement. You emphasized the need to stand very still behind the podium. You said it was because I didn't want to look like I was flinching from the confetti cannons, but instead it made me look fearless while bullets were flying through the air. Until Luca ushered me away and I was hit by a bullet ricochet."

Luca's head whipped over, his jaw dropping. He was putting it together too.

"I don't know how..." Megan sputtered. "Elizabeth! The fact that you would even entertain such a thought—"

"And here today," I interrupted. "What did you tell me on the steps of the Capitol Building, when I was afraid of walking out in the open? *Elizabeth. I want you to trust me. You are 100% safe right now. Nothing is going to happen to you.* That's what you said, Megan."

"Because I was trying to instill confidence in you!" she shouted. "Are you honestly accusing me of trying to have you assassinated? Me, your *campaign manager?*"

"Of course not," I said with a laugh that I didn't feel. "You didn't want me to be assassinated. You wanted it to *appear* like someone was trying to assassinate me. To generate attention, and media buzz, and everything else. That's why you were so tearfully apologetic in my office earlier—because you felt guilty that the fake assassination attempt almost got me killed for real. I've never seen you cry, Megan, not *once* in all our years working together. Tell me I'm wrong."

She looked scared, like she was about to break down in tears right now. The look in her eyes was the look of someone who was being falsely accused of something terrible. For a single heartbeat my certainty wavered.

Then the look disappeared, and was replaced with annoyance.

"I told you I would do whatever it takes to win," she said, hands on her hips. "That's literally what you pay me for. You don't want to know the slimy details because that would taint your perfect little campaign. It would ruin your spunky, valiant demeanor. I did all of this for you, and kept it secret so you would never have to get your hands dirty. So you could pretend like you were *pure.*"

My jaw dropped. "Are you blaming this on *me?*"

"Who else's fault is it!" she shouted. Anthony whipped his head around. "It's not mine, *Elizabeth*. So what if I hired someone to scare you at 4:00 in the morning, or put a few bullets into the Ohio Statehouse? I'm just the employee! I'm just doing what I was hired to do!"

Even though I knew it was true while accusing her, hearing her admit it was chilling. Some part of me didn't believe she was capable of this until I heard it from her own two lips.

"You're crazy," I said. "Legitimately crazy." Anthony and Ethan had realized something was wrong and were closing in behind Megan, slow and cautious in case she made any sudden moves.

My campaign manager gestured. "Look around, *senator*. All of this media attention and polling is a result of what I did. You stand there and lecture me? You should be giving me a raise! Not to mention it brought you three fuck-boy bodyguards."

My hand shot out all on its own, catching Megan across the cheek in a hard slap and knocking her sideways. Her eyes widened and she touched her cheek, which was already turning from white to scarlet.

"It's one thing to attack my character," I said, looming over her. "It's even understandable to attack my campaign strategy. But don't you *ever* attack these three men again. Unlike you, they've done nothing but protect me from danger. They would die for me."

"Fuckin' right we would," Anthony said. Ethan gave an emphatic nod and grabbed Megan's hands, restraining them behind her back. She didn't resist.

"Elizabeth," Megan begged. "You were never in any real danger! The mugger used blanks!"

"That's why forensics never recovered any bullets," Anthony said, realization spreading on his face.

"No danger?" I asked. "I was literally shot in Ohio!"

"You weren't supposed to move." Megan was becoming hysterical now that she realized it was all over. "The shooter was only spraying a few bullets into the marble columns! Nowhere near anyone else! Elizabeth! *I did it all for you!*"

She continued shouting while my bodyguards escorted her a safe distance away from the crowd, who was now watching curiously. Luca radio'd for the police to take Megan away.

Ethan put a reassuring hand on my back. "We'll deal with her later. You've got a speech to make."

I returned to the side of the stage, where one of the other senators was speaking. Pollock approached me before anyone else. "What was all that about?" he asked.

"My campaign manager and I had a political disagreement. Nothing to worry about."

He watched her being escorted away, but said nothing. "I trust she told you about my offer?"

"She did."

"I want to amend it," he said.

My heart sank. He was going to retract our cooperation agreement. Had my argument with Megan spooked him?

"Bob..." I began.

"Elizabeth," he lowered his voice, "I don't want to make you my VP at the end of the primary. I want to announce it right now, on President's Day. Here in front of all the press."

My mouth hung open. I closed it and said, "Nobody has ever announced their VP pick so early. Not in modern history."

"Exactly!" he said. "We would sweep the primaries! Nobody else would dare challenge us. And with our home states of Florida and Ohio locked up, it would be impossible for us to lose the general election."

The other senator was leaving the stage to a smattering of applause. Many of the photographers were aiming their cameras at me, preparing for my walk up onto the stage. "Bob, I have a speech already prepared..."

"Tack the announcement on to the end of it," he insisted. "Mention how you have something exciting to announce, then welcome me back on stage with you. We'll hold hands and tell them together."

A coordinator with a headset and a clipboard stuck her head into our conversation. "Senator O'Hare? I was told you'd like to make a speech before the event ends?"

"Go get 'em," Pollock said, pushing me toward the stage.

The crowd erupted in applause and camera clicks as I climbed the steps onto the stage. Luca went first, with Anthony close on my tail. Ethan remained behind by the steps and scanned the crowd for threats. My own little security detail. Three men who cared about me as much as I cared about them.

It made me feel safer than a hundred Secret Service agents.

I smiled and waved my way to the podium, and then waited another long moment for the noise to die down. The crowd, which had only occupied a small area before I arrived, now spread out in every direction. It was larger than the crowd at the Ohio Statehouse. Everyone was excited to hear what the missing senator had to say.

"Did you miss me?" I said into the microphone, which drew another roar from the crowd. I cleared my throat and launched into the speech Megan had prepared for me.

"It feels wonderful to be back on the Hill. By now, most of you know that there was an attack on my life last week. I've spent the past few days with a Secret Service detail. They insisted on keeping me safe from danger. Hidden away where nobody could find me, but also where I could not do my job.

"Well, I'm here on President's Day to announce that I'm done hiding. I'm done being afraid. If my candidacy terrifies my opponents so much, then that's proof I need to march forward without fear. It's proof I must work twice as hard to represent the people of this great country. It's proof that our cause is worth fighting for."

I paused for the crowd to cheer. Pollock was nodding at me from the stage steps, waiting to join me. It was time. This was it.

And in that moment, I made a decision.

39

Ethan

She was a lot of things. Ohio Senator Elizabeth O'Hare. Formerly Representative O'Hare from Ohio's Fifth District. A junior member of the Senate Finance Committee who was already making a name for herself grilling corrupt bankers. Now she was Elizabeth O'Hare, candidate for President of the United States.

But to me, she would always be the client with the mask. The one I'd fallen for in a hotel room before I'd ever seen her face. The one I had dreamed about before realizing who she was. The one I *still* dreamed about now that I knew the truth. Dreams of getting tangled in the sheets on lazy Saturday mornings, and of cooking breakfast while naked. Dreams where we smiled and laughed and were never apart.

The reality might not line up that way since she was running for president. But this woman? This intelligent, gorgeous, *incredible* woman? I'd take whatever I could get from her.

Even if that means sharing her with Anthony and Luca.

"She's something special, isn't she?"

I glanced at Senator Pollock. "She sure is."

"We're going to crush the competition," he promised. "Combining our campaigns into one ticket now is the smartest thing your boss has ever done."

But then Elizabeth surprised us.

"I would like to wish the other candidates best of luck on the trail," she said into the microphone. She turned to face Pollock. "Senator Pollock, hopefully we can keep things civil in the primary. But not *too* civil, especially regarding your stance on private prison reform. But in any case, may the best man—or woman—win!"

"What the fuck," Pollock growled.

She was doing it her way. She wasn't going to accept being Pollock's VP pick.

I couldn't stop smiling.

The crowd roared at the end of the speech and she spent several moments waving and smiling for the cameras. When she was finally escorted down the steps by Anthony and Luca, Pollock was practically crimson with anger.

"What happened?" he demanded. I carefully slid myself between him and Elizabeth, using my body as a barrier. One look at me and he took a step back. Only then did I step to the side again. "What about our deal?"

I admired the look in Elizabeth's eyes. She was calm and confident while staring down the rival senator.

She looked *presidential.*

"Senator Pollock," she said formally. "I've wanted to run for president since I was a little girl. It has been my core motivation at every stopping point along the way. And no matter what Megan, or you, or anyone else thinks is the most *prudent* political decision, I can't just run to be someone else's VP. I owe it to myself to shoot for the top."

Pollock's jaw hung open, revealing rows of too-white teeth. "I may not choose you as VP at the end of this! Not if you don't agree to this now."

"That's fair."

"Listen to me!" he insisted. "Don't you understand what you're giving up?"

"I understand completely," she said. Her voice was level. "But don't worry, Senator Pollock. When I win the primary, maybe I'll pick *you* as my running mate. So, you've got that to look forward to."

She strode off to the press area to begin

answering questions and giving interviews. I turned my smile on Pollock.

"You said it yourself: she's something special." I patted him on the arm. "Good luck with the rest of your campaign."

40

Elizabeth

For the first time in my life, I wasn't afraid.

I knew what I wanted. And, more importantly, what I *didn't* want. I didn't want to pretend to be someone I wasn't. I didn't want to launch this campaign with the intention of losing.

That was what had been missing in all of this. I was unmotivated at the thought of merely running for a VP spot on someone else's ticket. I wanted to run a legitimate campaign. I wanted to chase my dream. Even if it meant I would probably lose.

My three bodyguards formed up around me as I approached the press pen. It was totally natural for them. It felt natural for *me* to have them surrounding me at all times. It made me feel safe.

I steeled myself and began taking questions from reporters.

There were the obvious questions first. Where had I been while I was missing? Was I held against my will? Had the assassin been caught?

"I'm unaware of any progress of the investigation into my shooting," I said. "You'll have to speak with the investigators involved to get an update."

"Senator O'Hare! Do you feel safe?"

"Very safe," I said. I meant it, too.

"But how can you feel safe knowing the assassin is still out there?"

"I have the best bodyguards in the world keeping me safe around the clock."

Then there were a multitude of questions that should have been asked after the Ohio Statehouse speech. I was asked about my campaign focus, and what would be my top priority on day one if elected. I was asked if I would be raising money through a Political Action Committee, or if my campaign would be more grassroots-driven. Someone asked if my age was a concern.

"The people should vote for the best candidate to lead them," I said, "whether that person is 35 or 65."

"Senator, are you concerned about your love

life?"

The question jolted me unlike any of the others. "I found the reporter who had asked it and replied, "Can you clarify what you mean?"

"It's rare to see a politician who is unmarried," the reporter said. A grey-haired woman who looked judgmental. "Especially a female politician. Are you concerned that your single status will be seen as a negative among family voters?"

"I would hope the voters would care more about my policies on campaign finance reform more than the lack of a ring on this finger." I held up my hand.

"Follow up question! Are you presently seeing anyone? And if so, are you worried any love interests you might have would be unfairly scrutinized by the media and your opponents?"

My three bodyguards shifted their feet and glanced at me. I could feel the smiles from Anthony and Ethan, and the curious gaze of Luca while they waited for my answer.

It would have been easy to brush aside the question with a safe answer. It's what Megan would have told me to do. Say something vague about focusing on my campaign rather than my love life. But what I was quickly realizing was that I didn't want to do the *safe* thing, both in my campaign and in life. I had to be myself. I couldn't allow the world to dictate what I was and wasn't allowed to do.

The only person in control of my life was *me*.

I smiled back at the reporter, although the smile was meant for my three bodyguards. My three lovers. We were going to have a lot of fun on the campaign trail.

"I might see people," I said. "I might not. We'll see what happens. But ultimately, it's none of your business. As a female politician, I'm not going to allow my campaign to be distinguished by the men in my life. In fact, let's get all of the silly tabloid questions out of the way now."

I kept my demeanor calm, but there was a mocking edge to my tone.

"Who am I sleeping with? Whoever I want. Or is it *whomever*? Pretend I said it the correct way. Do I want a family and kids? Sure, maybe someday, but I'm a little more focused on my campaign at the moment. How much time do I spend every day on my hair and makeup? Way too much." I rolled up my right sleeve and held my arm up for everyone to see. "I've got some tattoos here. Better to get a good look at them now instead of trickling bits and pieces of what you see out in the tabloids. The birds flying up my fingers represent freedom, and perseverance. I got them in college. Yes, I've considered having them removed. No, I don't think it's important enough to worry about."

The reporters were all laughing by the time I was done. So were my bodyguards. But they also looked proud.

"Anything else?" I asked with my best smile. "Good. Now who has a *real* question for me? I don't know if you all heard, but I'm running for president."

My three bodyguards all grinned to themselves as I continued taking questions.

Epilogue

Elizabeth
21 Months Later

I paced in the hotel room, kicked off my heels, then paced some more.

"It's fine," Anthony said from the couch.

"You don't know that," I said.

He stood and blocked my pacing path. He wore a slim-fitting grey suit that covered up most of his tattoos, though the top of one still peaked out above his shirt collar. His tie was jet black and matched his belt and shoes. All in all, the former USCP cop cleaned up *real* nice.

He removed the ear piece from his ear. The one that connected him—and my other bodyguards—to my legitimate Secret Service detail. Then he gripped me by the forearms and rubbed them up and down like he was trying to keep me warm.

"You're right, I don't know if it's fine. But there's no point in worrying about it now."

"I completely disagree," I said. "This is the *perfect* time to worry about it."

"Elizabeth..." he said gently.

"I'm worrying because worrying is all I have to do."

"I know."

It was strange not having anything on my schedule. I hadn't had more than an hour of free time to myself in the past 20 months. It should have been nice. Relaxing.

Instead, it made me antsy.

Anthony hugged me close. He was wearing cologne tonight, a special occasion. The Burberry Indigo I'd bought him for his birthday, based on the citrus-and-wood scent. I breathed deep and let his strong arms make me feel safe.

"You shouldn't worry," he said. "I think you're going to—"

"Don't say it!" I glared at him. "You'll jinx it."

"I didn't think you believed in jinxes."

"I don't. But tonight isn't the time to tempt fate, now is it?"

The door to the bedroom lurched as weight was thrown against it, shaking on its hinges. Both of us whipped our heads toward it.

"We can't keep him in there forever," Anthony said.

"Luca insisted. Besides, we need him for later."

As if to emphasize the point, the door shook again, followed by shouting from Ethan inside. Trying to give commands.

"Ethan's got it taken care of," I said.

"And I've got *you* taken care of." Anthony got a silly grin on his face.

"Anyone could walk in," I said.

"That's what makes it fun."

He grabbed a handful of my ass and kissed me hard. I opened my mouth for him and reached for the front of his suit, feeling the growing bulge within. Even after almost two years together I could make him hard at the drop of a hat. Likewise, his tongue inside my mouth made me instantly wet, especially with his hand sliding under my skirt and up my bare cheek, fingers digging into my ass...

A knock came at the front door of my suite. With practiced form, Anthony and I parted and stood next to each other as if nothing were amiss. Luca's weathered face appeared in the doorway. "Ma'am? Senator Pollock is here to speak with you."

I cleared my throat and smoothed out of skirt. "Send him in."

Bob Pollock strode inside like he owned the place. There was a dour expression on his tan face.

"What is it?" I asked. "What do you know?"

Suddenly a silly grin invaded his face. "They're about to call Pennsylvania for you."

"No freaking way!" I whirled toward the television. It was muted, but the anchor was currently showing a breakdown of exit polling data from North Carolina. "They just said only 50% of precincts are reporting."

"I just got a call from my buddy on the state election board. All the Pittsburgh precincts are coming in now, and the results are *very* good."

"How good? We already knew Pittsburgh would tip the scales in our favor. Are we talking 25 points up? Or closer to 30?"

"Elizabeth!" Anthony suddenly said. "Look!"

We all turned back toward the television while he turned up the volume. There was a whirl of BREAKING NEWS graphics, ending with a map of Pennsylvania that covered the screen.

"*Based on our current projections, we are ready to call the state of Pennsylvania for O'Hare.*" A picture of my headshot faded into view over the state, which then changed colors on the main map.

Someone shouted in the hallway.

"Wait," I said. I was trying to do the mental math for the remaining electoral votes. We hadn't expected Pennsylvania to get called so early in the night. "What does this mean?"

Senator Pollock, my running mate and ally, extended his hand. "Congratulations, Elizabeth. The people have just elected you the next President of the United States."

We embraced and I clenched my eyes shut. I couldn't believe it.

After all these months, we'd *won*.

"I need to go tell my family, but I wanted to let you know first," Pollock said. "Trevor will let us know when it's time to go downstairs and make your victory speech." For one more moment he held my eyes. "You did it, Elizabeth."

"*We* did it," I corrected.

He grinned and went back out into the hall, where people were beginning to shout with excitement. Luca slipped inside and let the door close behind him. "Is it true?"

Anthony only pointed at the television. The Electoral College total had incremented up to 274, which was above the 269 mark required.

"It's not official until the western states report in—"

I cut off as Luca hugged me. "You did it," he whispered into my hair.

"*We* did it. Is everyone forgetting how this was a team effort? I'm not a one-woman campaign."

"You're kind of the centerpiece, though," Anthony said.

The door to the bedroom lurched again, with the sound of wood cracking in the frame.

"Oh for Pete's sake," Luca said. He raised his voice and added, "Let him out!"

"But the deposit for the room," Anthony warned.

"Fuck the deposit," I said. "We can all celebrate."

The door to the bedroom opened and Boomer came charging out like a racehorse. He put his paws up on my chest and leaned up to lick at my face. I protested and squealed and pushed him off.

"Boomer, no!" Ethan said, following from the bedroom. His own suit was disheveled and his tie was loose. His surfer hair looked even more chaotic than normal. "What about the hotel deposit?" he asked Luca.

"Elizabeth says fuck the deposit," Anthony said.

"Correction," Luca said. "The *President-Elect* says fuck the deposit."

"Don't jinx it!" Ethan hissed.

Anthony pointed at the television.

Ethan's eyes became round marbles. "Is that legit? That has to be a mistake. I thought we wouldn't know for sure until the west coast polls closed!"

"Pennsylvania swung our way," I said. "That changed all the math. It's over."

Ethan had tears in his eyes as he embraced me. "I knew you could do it," he whispered. "I always knew."

I squeezed him tighter and felt tears welling up in my own eyes. "If you make me cry and my mascara runs, the makeup girl is going to pitch a fit."

Anthony and Luca joined in the group hug on the other side, surrounding me with their warmth and love. Nobody said anything. We just savored the moment together. Peaceful and silent.

We all knew that soon things would get even crazier than they'd been for the past two years.

I'd hired Ethan and Anthony on as my full-time bodyguards. Even though my campaign manager Megan was arrested and quietly charged with a dozen crimes, Luca remained my Secret Service detail up until I won my party's primary. After that I was given a *full* Secret Service detail of a dozen rotating agents, but I still kept my two bodyguards as well.

Having them by my side through all of this made everything easier. The guys didn't mind sharing me, especially since our schedules varied depending on the day. On Monday morning I might have Luca and Anthony watching me, and then Ethan would take over for Anthony in the afternoon. And despite how hectic the campaign trail was, we found the energy at night to have some *extra* fun together. Whether it was in twos, or threes, or occasionally even all four of us, it just sort of *worked*. Nobody complained about our unusual relationship.

Ethan, Anthony, and Luca seemed happy to share. It made me happy, too.

Could we keep it going while I was POTUS, though?

"What happens next?" Ethan asked softly.

"She has to make a victory speech," Luca explained. "Then the transition team takes over, working with the existing administration to—"

"No," Ethan said. "I mean what happens next with *us*?"

The three of them looked to me.

"I don't know what will happen," I admitted. "But I do know one thing: I want to make it work."

"Can you, though?" Anthony asked.

I gave him a look. "I'm about to become the most powerful woman in the world. If I can't make it work, nobody can."

Someone knocked on the front door. The four

of us spread apart quickly so whoever came in wouldn't see our intimate moment.

Vice President-Elect Pollock poked his head through the door. "They don't want you to make a victory speech until the west coast polls close. But as soon as they do, be ready to give the people downstairs what they want."

"I've got it all ready," I said. "Waiting will whip them up into a frenzy. It'll be a killer speech."

"I know it will," he said with a proud smile, then ducked out.

Luca went to the door and poked his head outside. After speaking to the agent by the door he came back inside.

"What'd you tell him?"

"That the *President-Elect* is going to rest for half an hour, and that she doesn't wish to be disturbed."

I raised an eyebrow. "You're dictating my nap schedule?"

His shrug was nonchalant. "Not necessarily a nap. Just laying down for a few minutes."

"Resting your eyes," Anthony said, putting a hand on my back. His lips found my neck, kissing gently.

"You're not just our boss anymore," Ethan said in front of me. "Now you're our *leader*. Like, of our entire country."

I sighed under Anthony's kisses, which were moving lower to my shoulder. "I suppose that turns you on?"

"Fuck yeah it does," Anthony said.

Luca nodded slyly. "Power is attractive."

I let them guide me to the bedroom, where they slowly undressed me and tossed my clothes aside. That was fine—I had a totally separate outfit picked out for my victory speech. Luca went down on me on the edge of the bed while Anthony sucked on one of my nipples. Ethan kissed me on the mouth while Luca's tongue swirled around my clit, melting away all the stress and anxiety from election day. One finger slid into my pussy, followed by a second, then third.

Soon I was moaning into Ethan's mouth. He kept his lips on mine in a long kiss to muffle my cries of pleasure while I squirmed on the bed, held down by their six strong, forceful hands.

"More," I breathed when I came down from my shuddering climax. "I want all of you."

Luca took my pussy, spreading my legs wide while fucking me on the edge of the bed. I stroked Ethan's cock while Anthony went to his knees next to my head, turning me sideways so he could fuck my mouth. Ethan grabbed the back of my head and pushed me down on his fellow bodyguard, forcing his shaft deeper into my mouth.

It was pure sexual bliss. Rarely did all three of us find time to be together like this. It was exactly what I needed near the end of the biggest day of my life.

"Oh my God," Luca moaned as he crashed his cock into my cunt as hard as he could. "Fuck! Oh fuck!"

"Give me your come," I breathed, stroking Ethan and Anthony with each of my hands. "I want it!"

"I want to give. It. To. *Youuuu*..."

His face twisted with ecstasy as he shot his load deep inside of me, a beautiful trembling spasm from his cock that vibrated against my inner walls.

He pulled out and came around to kiss me, and Anthony eagerly took his place between my legs. He was a god of muscle and tattoo ink as he spread my legs wide and slid inside my waiting lips. Within moments he was breathing fast and coming inside me in long, fluid strokes, adding his seed to Luca's.

"Give me yours," I told Ethan. Commanded. "Your President-Elect demands it."

"Yes ma'am."

As he slid inside I grabbed a handful of his blond hair and pulled him down into a kiss, because I wanted to feel his body against mine as he filled me. Our tongues danced and swirled as he made deep love to me, coming within seconds just like the others.

By the time we quickly cleaned up and dressed there was a knock at the door. I stayed in the bedroom to touch up my makeup while a freshly-clothed Luca went to the door.

"Who was that?" I asked when he came back.

"They don't care about the west coast," he said. "They want your victory speech *now*. Apparently the crowd is going nuts down there."

I reapplied my Ruby Woo lipstick and stood from the desk. "Then we'd better give them what they want. Keep your eyes peeled. Now I'm an even *bigger* target than before."

"Of course, ma'am," Luca said.

"You got it," Ethan added.

Anthony nodded. "We'll watch your back, sugar." He gave my ass a hard slap as an exclamation point.

I smiled at the three of them. My lovers. My bodyguards.

The men I *loved*.

No matter what the future held, we would find a way to stay together.

They formed up around me in a protective arc, and we went downstairs to greet my roaring constituents.

Cassie Cole is a Reverse Harem Romance writer living in Norfolk, Virginia. A polygamist/polyamorist at heart, she thinks Romance is best when served in threes, fours, and fives!

If you'd like to receive info on new releases and special deals, you can sign up for Cassie's newsletter here:

http://eepurl.com/dFpnSz

Books by Cassie Cole

Broken In

Drilled

Five Alarm Christmas

All In
Triple Team
Shared by her Bodyguards

Printed in Great Britain
by Amazon